# SOLD OUT

# SOLD OUT

## 99 % POSSIBLY TRUE STORIES OF CLASS WARFARE

### ANGELA KAUFMAN

Published by Trash Panda Press

ISBN 978-1-7362544-5-5

Typesetting services by BOOKOW.COM

# PREFACE

**Class Traitor**- a person who is a member of the proleteriate who works against their own class interest intentionally or otherwise.

# Acknowledgments

This is a work of fiction. Any relationship to recognizable events is proof of the prevalence of classism that we have been living.

But what good is the evidence and what good is the argument? They are determined to kill us regardless of evidence, of law, of decency, of everything. If they give us a delay tonight, it will only mean they will kill us next week.
Nicola Sacco, August 22, 1927

# Downwardly Mobile

## December 2020

### Rob

Rob pulls the mail truck to the side of Route 9P. The scenic road wraps around Saratoga Lake before leading into Saratoga Springs.

The trailer park is his last stop before the long holiday weekend. A weekend that can't come soon enough. He lifts the mailbag, lighter than it was before, and waits for traffic to slow so he can step outside of the truck. On the side of the road, the mailboxes are lined up and hungry. All fifteen of them. Minus the empty lot. Nails protrude from the crooked wooden frame, missing mailbox languishing in a snowbank on the ground below.

Behind him, the mail truck's radio emits Christmas classics. He hums along.

*We wish you a merry Christmas… we wish you a merry…*

Rob digs through the bag, starting at the mailbox marked Lot One. The Duncans have a stack today. A Discover card bill sticks out of the pile of letters. A small package, a Christmas present coming just in time? Also, a local Penny Saver and a certified letter. Rob notices the return address. Hometown

Realty. He's seen it before. The company owns this small trailer park.

The park sprawling back behind trees, far behind the row of mailboxes partially concealed from the main road. He looks up then. Catching sight of the few visible trailers. Sloping roofs. Missing skirting. Mismatched siding.

Rob knows each home. He knows the families that live here, and not just through eyeing their mail day after day.

Once you end up here there's nowhere else to go.

*We wish you a merry Christmas....*

Rob grabs the bundle for the next mailbox. Then for Lot Three.

*Good tidings we bring, to you and your kin.*

Each of 'em has the same certified letter. Hometown Realty. Each with a receipt of delivery requested.

Lot Six, the trailer where Dave and his wife have lived for years. Nice people, a bit strange, but who isn't? A bill from the garbage company. Letter from the car insurance company. Utility bill. Another certified letter.

*Good tidings for Christmas and a Happy New Year....*

Lot Seven. Brandi. She's a hot mess, that one. Left all alone raising those two kids. The older, a girl, has a funny name. Jayden. Younger kid, Danny. There's a letter from the Saratoga County Mental Health clinic. Rob tries not to look but can't help it. Then a Citi card bill, and the plump square shape of a greeting card. This one addressed to the whole family. Even has the name of their dog on it, Baxter.

Return address Saratoga Springs. Same last name. Maybe a greeting card from an aunt or grandmother. Over on the better side of the tracks.

For them, too the same certified letter.

*Now bring us some figgy pudding, now bring us some figgy pudding…*

Lot Eight. Francis Green. Letter from unemployment. That's new, Rob thought he recalled Francis working at the manufacturing plant a few exits down on the Northway. He hadn't heard of the plant closing down, but if it did, well, that's too bad. And this time of year, no less. An envelope from the Foundation for Mercy, probably asking for a tithing. Another of the same certified letters.

There's one for Lot Nine, Rob thinks with growing curiosity and unease. Nice family, got a little kid. Another name Rob has never heard of for a first name until, well, probably until that kid was born. Grafton. Like the lake in Rensselaer County. He's seen them a time or two walking with their older dog to get the mail. Precocious kid. Always asking questions.

*We wish you a merry Christmas and a happy new year!*

The song finishes and Rob is just about to put the last of the mail into the few remaining boxes. Ads. Bills. And each a copy of the same certified letter.

He fills the last box, Lot Fifteen, with mail for Chuck and his wife, Donna. Hospital bills again. Must be every week there's another. Makes sense, she was real sick for a while. In the hospital on and off, Rob recalls from conversations with Chuck. A paystub for Chuck from InteroTech. And another of those dang certified letters.

Rob walks back to the truck and hauls himself into the front seat. He blasts the heat and rubs his chapped hands together. Through the side window, frost slowly gives way to fog. When he can see enough of the run-down park through his passenger side window, and the abandoned motel across the street through his driver's side window, it's time to give the winding road behind him one last look before pulling onto the road.

"Can't be good," he says aloud to himself as he drives across the two-lane bridge that stretches over Saratoga Lake. Whatever business the landlord's about it can't be good.

## Jerry

### 1/10/2021

The sun has barely risen over Saratoga Lake, their favorite time for a stroll. The shoulder along the road is narrow. Strategic planning intended to discourage foot traffic. Jerry read that in an article online. Not to be deterred, the couple meanders in and out of the side streets off of Route 9P, the landscape is dotted with modest homes and seasonal camps.

On the other side of the bridge, a sign proudly proclaims Regatta View Drive. Sizable homes with sturdy foundations dug deep into pristine lawns. But not here. On this side of the bridge, such opulence is out of reach. On this side of the bridge, the couple walks through neighborhoods closer to their own stratosphere.

If anyone had asked Jerry what he thought of poverty porn, he'd be offended by the notion of better off people taking walking tours through downtrodden neighborhoods.

The thought doesn't occur to him today, as they take in the sights of the trailer park off the main road. Jerry studies the spectacles surrounding them. He pulls at the waxed tip of his pointed goatee with one hand, stretching it below his mask, twisting the edge of his curled mustache through the side of the cloth face covering.

Mobile homes that were old when Reaganomics was new. Held together with tape and resignation. One with front steps missing. Another with tape covering cracks in a window. Some are adorned with Christmas lights and wreaths. Appliances and seemingly random hardware blockade the tiny lots.

Lois swats Jerry's hand away from his mustache. She used to tease him about looking like the Pringles' logo, but since the pandemic hit last spring, she's been begging him to shave it off.

"Stop that, you're going to spread germs!" she insists.

Lois drops her hand to his, squeezing it tighter as her eyes wander from one sagging roof to another. Knowing better than to speak the words out loud, secretly feeling superior as she thinks of her home.

Jerry takes in the view as well. Strolling arm in arm with his wife just enjoying the calm.

"When we head back, I think I'll stop into Stewart's for some coffee," Lois tells him, lowering her mask just long enough to apply her Chapstick

"Yeah, I could grab some…"

"My God! Jerry! Look!" She points into the distance. Jerry, who had been watching squirrels run across the road, almost missed it. Though now, he can't imagine how he didn't see it sooner.

A man with stooped shoulders and greying hair stands on a step ladder outside of a battered mobile home. His back is to them as he fusses with a tree limb. The morning fog is still dissipating. It takes a moment for Jerry's eyes to adjust. It takes longer for him to realize what the man is doing. The reason for his wife's sudden reaction.

Yes, indeed. The man is tying a noose. Around here, a white man hanging rope on a tree limb can mean one of two things.

"Hey!" Jerry calls out to him, letting go of Lois's arm and walking toward the man.

The man startles and drops the rope, gripping the ladder to brace himself. He slowly backs down one step, then another, until he's on solid ground. His hands are shaking as he bows his head slightly. His ears turn bright red and his eyes dart to the side. Jerry thinks he looks like he's just been caught stealing.

"What's all this?" Jerry asks motioning to the noose, now hanging awkwardly- incomplete and sloppy looking.

The man leans heavily on the ladder, still avoiding eye contact. He points to the trailer. "This is all I had," he begins. "Been here for twenty years." He raises both hands to the sides of his head. "Twenty years. And they're selling the park."

Jerry nods and the man continues. Hands on his hips now, jaw set in a line halfway between desperation and simmering anger. "New owner said he's gonna shut it down."

He looks Jerry in the face now and for the first time, Jerry sees how red the man's eyes are. "

"Twenty years!" he keeps shaking his head, repeating the phrase like a mantra.

Jerry feels Lois's hand on his arm. He lets his breath out in a long sigh and shakes his head in sympathy.

"Twenty years! I'm too tired. Too old to start over. Broke. And too damn tired."

He pounds his fists on the ladder with each word of this last statement, as if it was the ladder that had robbed him.

Jerry nods his head slowly, thinking the man looks how he too would look if he stayed out late, got fucked up, beat up, and shot up.

"I can't even think of trying to start over."

"Indeed," Jerry begins. Lois cuts in.

"But it's a permanent solution to a temporary problem."

Jerry winces. He knows Lois means well, but her words ring hollow.

"Temporary?" the man laughs, "is where DSS will stick me. Motel, shelter," he shakes his head at the thought of the marathon of impermanence that awaits. "No. It's all too much. I've got nothing now." He gestures to the other homes. "Gonna close the park. Turn it into boat storage."

Jerry notices that as he says this, the man's back is now to the noose. He's taken a few steps away from the ladder.

*He needs someone to just listen. Maybe best to keep him talking.*

"You know what I used to do? For thirty years?" he asks.

"No, what was that?" Jerry asks, trying to keep eye contact.

"Manufacturing!" He raises his hands in the air again, *Greatest Show on Earth* style, and then bellows with laughter. "Made the boats! Hurt my back doing it. Can't work anymore" he pounds his chest and points toward the lake. "I made their damn boats. Now they take my damn home."

He's yelling now. Jerry thinks this is good. Anger requires energy. Motivation. Self-preservation.

"Is that so? And on a disability income, that's only what, two grand a month?" Jerry ventures a guess.

"Two grand? I wish! When all was said and done with worker's comp, I get twelve-sixty."

Jerry's jaw drops behind his mask. No wonder the guy wants to hang himself. "Gonna be hard to find a rental on that income," he agrees. "Unbelievable. Criminal, even." Jerry lowers his tone. "Listen, if you do this," he gestures to the noose, "if you do this, here all alone like this, you're missing an opportunity."

The man squints. He looks confused but leans in, listening. Jerry continues.

"All I'm saying is, if you're sure this is the end for you, why do it this way? Alone? Don't you realize the capitalist machine will just keep on rolling? It probably won't even make the news. If you end up with nothing either way, why not go out fighting?"

"Jerry!" Lois scolds. Jerry doesn't break his momentum. He continues.

"This greedy bastard is throwing you out on the streets to build a storage place for boats. That's not a good look."

The man strokes his chin with his index finger while nodding his head slowly. He nods, reaching out a hand in Jerry's direction. "Name's Fran. After St. Francis," he points with his free hand to a Saint's medal worn around his neck.

"Well, I'm Jerry. This is Lois," he pauses for a moment and then adds, "not to get too personal, but a Catholic like yourself wouldn't want to, uh, jeopardize things with your eternal soul, right? Or at least would want to make it worth the effort. Really make a statement."

"A statement." Fran echoes.

"Right," Lois says, "Just ask yourself 'what would Jesus do?'"

"I 'spose," the man begins, calmer now, "he would walk up to someone like this businessman, knock his furniture all over the place, and tell him to go to Hell."

"Damn right!" Jerry gives an encouraging fist pump.

"I'll give this some thought." Fran nods his head. Jerry notices a spark of light in his eyes, as if he's having an epiphany.

"Don't let him get away with this. If you kill yourself, not only does he win, but no one will even know what's happening here, don't go out quietly."

The older man looks off into the distance, a smile slowly spreads across his face.

* * *

## Jerry

Jerry surveys the Marina across the street, his back to Stewart's. He doesn't notice at first when Lois returns to meet him in the parking lot.

"You shouldn't have encouraged him," she says.

"Encourage him? He was tying a noose. I didn't have to encourage him. I'm just helping him make the statement he wants to make on his, uh, way out."

She shakes her head as they stroll down 9P and over the bridge, heading toward the greener pastures of Saratoga Springs.

"Still, most people with a conscience would try to talk a man off a ledge."

"When you find a person with a conscience, do let me know."

"Why? So you can drive him off a cliff and make it to go viral?"

\* \* \*

12/25/2020

## Chuck LOT 15

Chuck hears the sound from the television. Jimmy Stewart wishing the movie house a Merry Christmas. Donna's favorite, this is the third time she's watched it this week. He sighs, eyeing the open door, a soft glow from the Christmas tree cast into the bedroom where he sits, alone, trying to finish topping off some extra work.

But he can't focus on the laptop that rests on a small tray. The kind that was meant for breakfasts in bed that will never happen.

"It's Christmas, Chuck, try to relax and just enjoy our last Christmas here, ok?" Donna calls into him from the living room.

Chuck grabs the stack of medical bills collected by his side. He opens a drawer in the bedside stand and pushes the papers down. For good measure, he places a planner and a few stray notebooks over the medical bills, concealing them completely, should Donna open the drawer. Not that she would.

The new growing pile of papers bring the tally to over one hundred thousand dollars, even with insurance.

*I should go out there. Sit by the tree. Hold her hand.*

But he can't yet.

"I'll be right there," he says, and not for the first time this evening. He looks back to the screen on his laptop. Every word he tries to read oozes in his mind, turning to nothing. He can't concentrate.

He leans his head from side to side, cracking his neck. On the walls, posters from his favorite bands conceal a paint job that's aged about as well as his midlife physique. The jam bands he followed in college. The rock bands he idolized as a teen. The Jazz musicians that made him want to learn saxophone. Long ago when he and Donna first married. And were both able to work.

"Chuck, it's Christmas," Donna calls to him again. Chuck closes his eyes. He tries to keep his voice level. To not ruin the evening. Again.

"Yeah, I bet Bonvenuto is having a great Christmas with his new real estate acquisition."

"Chuck, come on out here and have some eggnog!"

He's just about to log out of his virtual worksite and the job board. Donna can't find out he's looking for a second job. She can't find out how bad things are.

That's when a headline catches his eyes.

### Police Respond to Bomb Explosion in Nashville

Chuck barely remembers Christmas. New Year came and went in a fog. He knew it wasn't going to be the same. Between the virus and the other bad news. He sits now scouring through job listings. Hoping a side job will bring in enough extra money. Trying to recall the zoom visit with his kids and the grandkids. Ashamed that he had been barely able to follow what they were going on about.

"Grandpa, we got a puppy," his granddaughter, April, had said. Had he even responded? Had he cooed and shared in her excitement? He can't even remember what the puppy looked like. He was beginning to forget what his family looked like.

All he could think about was how much more was being taken away.

For days he had been operating on coffee and autopilot, a caffeinated haze of routines. Not wanting to tempt himself by thinking too much, while not being able to suppress what had begun lurking in the back of his mind.

"We got time; I don't know why you're worried. We'll figure somethin' out." Donna tries to reassure him.

*You don't know how bad things are.*

"Legal aid says he has to give us two years," Donna reminds him.

He wants to reply but can't.

He doesn't want to stress her. With her emphysema, and everything else. He has done his research. What else could he do now that sleep was out of the question? Their home, like most in this park, is too old to be relocated. Whether they lose everything in a year or in a week, the result is the same.

It was the third day, maybe the fourth, that he had the idea. Or the beginnings of it. The inspiration hit him, as inspiration often does, through music. A song. The day he heard on the news that the man who was now being called the Nashville Bomber had not just blown up an RV, with himself in it. He had also recorded a warning message to keep others away. A warning that the vehicle was going to explode. And there was something more.

The man in Nashville, Nash, as Chuck now thinks of him, had rigged the RV to serenade the neighborhood before exploding. He'd set it up to play *Downtown* by Petula Clark.

He thinks about it a lot since he got the letter about the park. Today another letter had come in the mail. About his term life policy, which would be expiring in a few months. He had only one option left to take care of his wife.

*One hundred grand, too bad I'm worth more dead than alive.*

\* \* \*

## January 2021

## Jayden LOT 7

Jayden's feet echo on the bare hardwood floors. Not like the worn carpet at her mom's trailer.

*When can we go back home? Is it even still there?*

She walks through the hall from the guest bedroom where she and Danny have been staying. Feeling the crisp white walls under her fingertips, she remembers her grandmother's harsh scolding from yesterday and pulls her hands to her side, not wanting Grandma to yell at her again.

No need to worry, she sees now. Grandma isn't watching her. She's watching the TV. It's huge. Takes up the whole wall. Like being in a movie theater.

That's one thing she could come to like about Grandma's house. If she ever got to watch a movie she wanted. Grandma's watching her new obsession. The Queen's Gambit. It's a boring old people's show.

Jayden looks around the dining room that blends in with the living room and kitchen. An open floor plan that makes Jayden feel like she's in a giant white cave. Well lit. Spacious. Suffocating.

Not like her home. A single-wide trailer by Saratoga Lake. Her home, where the front door spills into the living room. Where the walls are smoke-stained, and the wallpaper outdated but familiar, covered in some places by family photos, her drawings, and cool things like Christmas lights that Mom leaves up all year long.

In her home, you can wear your shoes if you want. There's a stain on the carpet where Baxter, their dog, threw up last year. Her home is drafty in the winter.

"That's why we have blankets," Mom says when Danny complains.

At her own home, you can put your feet on the couch. You can watch fun shows. Even if it is on a small TV.

Jayden's grandmother lives in Saratoga Springs. A Five-minute drive to a different world. This house is heated but cold. Clean and sterile. You have to tiptoe and not make noise. If you bump into something on accident, you can break it and get in trouble.

Jayden hates it when she and Danny have to stay here. Like last time. She wonders how long it will be now. She sits on a chair at the kitchen table, pulls scrap paper toward her, takes a pencil, and silently starts to draw.

Her mind wanders as she thinks about her home, and Mom. Everything was finally getting better. They even got to have Christmas this year, with her and Danny each getting a few presents. At thirteen, it had been a long time since she believed in Santa. She knew not to expect gifts. But getting them once in a while when Mom had money was a nice surprise. She had to keep up the lie for Danny, and that was hard. One year, when

Mom had been laid off, she told Danny Santa was sick with the flu and couldn't visit. It worked until he went to school and heard what Santa brought to other kids.

Oops.

She runs her pencil along the paper, sketching a family photo from memory. She remembers the last time she was home a week ago.

In the morning things were fine. In the afternoon, everyone was happy. Mom was still sober and had logged onto her Zoom NA meeting. Jayden had heard her mom say she had ninety-seven days that day. Things were improving.

Until Mom had gotten the letter.

Jayden had been on Zoom for math class, trying in vain to concentrate. Danny kept running around making noise.

"Shut up or I'll tell Mom to take away the game you got from Santa!" But her threat hadn't deterred him.

"I'm telling Mom when she gets back!" Jayden yelled again.

*She should have been back by now.*

Jayden thinks of that night last week and how her anxiety crept up as she watched the clock. It should have only taken five minutes to walk to the mailbox, at most ten if Mom stopped to talk to someone. When twenty minutes went by, Jayden started to obsessively check her phone, tuning out the teacher at that point.

No texts.

Jayden had even gone to the window to watch. In case she saw Mom's dealer's car pull up again.

That's when she heard the screaming. Followed by sobbing. Jayden pressed closer to the window and strained her eyes to catch sight of her mother walking down the road. As her mom approached the entry, Jayden ran back to the computer. Pretending to pay attention to class. Danny heard the commotion too. He looked like he was going to start whimpering.

"Shut up!" Jayden hissed at him.

He did.

That's when Mom had come in and slammed the door.

"Fucking Class Traitor! No good fucking Class Traitor!" Her mother had yelled.

Jayden has replayed the entire scene several times in the week that had passed. She can see it with no effort now, as she sits at her grandmother's table in this silent, cavernous house. Drawing circles with her pencil, around and around, filling in the dark center of her mother's eye as she remembers being careful to stay out of the way. How she watched her mother slam the mail down on the table and disappear into the bathroom.

And when she hadn't come out a half-hour later, it had been Jayden who called Grandma. And 911. Again.

She had known better than to interrupt her mother when she was yelling. Just like she knows better than to interrupt her grandmother when her shows are on.

She hears the show's theme song begin, another episode over. Tentatively, she slips out of her chair, careful not to scrape it on the fancy floor, and walks to the living room.

"Grandma, What's a Class Traitor?"

"Where on Earth did you hear that?" her grandmother asks, turning in the oversized sectional couch. Her glasses are held in place by a string of different colored beads, and as her grandmother eyes her, she pulls the glasses from her face, as if she needs to adjust her vision to hear Jayden's answer.

Jayden shrugs.

"Did you hear that on some liberal talk show?" Grandma asks, still holding the eyeglasses pensively in midair. It reminds Jayden of someone pointing an accusing finger.

"Yeah, I guess," she answers. "Are we losing our trailer?" Jayden asks then, already knowing the answer. She had read the letter while waiting for the ambulance. It was confusing, but Jayden had understood the one part.

"Don't know yet," Grandma says, turning back to the TV as another episode cues up. She sets her glasses delicately back on the bridge of her nose and crosses her arms.

*I hate it when she does this.*

Her grandmother continues, "for now, you and Danny are fine living here."

Jayden isn't reassured. She doesn't mind a sleepover. But she hates staying long. Like last time Mom was in rehab. Jayden feels a soft push on her knee. Baxter, their pit bull, is sitting patiently, waiting for a treat.

Grandma doesn't like Baxter, Jayden thinks. She wonders what will happen if they have to stay a long time.

Jayden wonders about being homeless again. And about Class Traitors. And if the two are related.

\* \* \*

## Chuck LOT 15

In all their years of marriage, Chuck has never lied to his wife. Never kept secrets from her. Until now. He leans close to her as she sits on her favorite recliner.

"I'll be back before dinner," Chuck says, as he kisses Donna.

Driving to Wal-Mart for supplies, he can see the scene playing out in his mind, inspired by the news of the Nashville bomber. Chuck knows it's sick, this odd inspiration that consumes his waking moments. What is he becoming?

He thought of the news reports. About how the guy sat in the RV while Petula Clark's *Downtown* played over and over again on a loudspeaker before the grand finale. Did some damage.

That's all he wants. Not to kill anyone. Or at least not anyone else. Donna will be hurt, yes, but his life insurance policy will ensure she is well taken care of.

As for Bonvenuto, he just wants to hit a rich man where it hurts. Right in his boats.

*I'm sorry Donna, I don't want to leave you here alone. But there's only enough for one of us to live. May as well let it be you.*

Of course, he has to use a different song. Can't be a copycat.

In his head, he hears the song. The Chambers Brothers. The most perfect piece of music that was almost never recorded. He's long thought so. Even tried to convince the guys in his old college band.

He can hear the psychedelic opening, the voices slightly echoing, a reminder that time has come today. He'll park the car outside Bonvenuto's current boat storage unit. The one next to the trailer park. Far enough away to not hurt anyone. Close enough to make a mark.

He imagines the scene. How music will blast from the speakers. It'll bug the shit out of the people sitting comfortably in their permanent homes.

He imagines the song repeating. Disrupting the peace, like an unwanted visitor, prying into their quiet Sunday afternoon.

*Let it play on a loop for a few hours. That's what Mr. Nashville must've done. Wasn't it, Nash?*

They may even call in a report. Probably not to the property owner. Just the cops. No love lost there. Not anymore. After all, the Sheriff will be the one who knocks on the door to serve the eviction in time.

*Has come today....*

Chuck runs through the list of supplies in his mind. Black powder, piping, some nails, a few kitchen timers.

When it's all over, people will know why. His reputation will take a hit but he won't be around to care.

"He worked in IT, just like the Nashville bomber," they'll say. They may even interview his coworkers at InteroTech. And they'll look at all the signs they shouldn't have missed. Maybe they'll consider the obvious. Chuck knows that's not guaranteed.

He starts singing to himself, tapping the steering wheel in the absence of a cowbell.

*Cuckoo.*

Catchy tune.

He pulls into Wal Mart. *No place left to run....*

When Chuck gets out of the car, he's whistling, still hearing the song in his head.

*I have no home.*


Had any cops pulled Chuck over on the way home from Wal-Mart, a quick sweep of a flashlight through the window would have revealed bags filled with all the loot he needs to rig his car full of explosives.

When the time comes.

*Time....*

But no one pulled him over. He made it home. As he pulls into the driveway, he notices his neighbor, Dave, lingering outside his house.

*Not now, dammit.*

Chuck pulls a moving blanket over his contraband before stepping out of the car.

"You get your letter?" Dave asks.

"Yep. Sonofabitch." Chuck bothers to pronounce the term, mostly because Dave is given to using the variation "sombitch." They may be neighbors, but Chuck knows he's nothing like Dave. Still, he tries to play nice. "Can you believe it?"

Dave walks over to Chuck's driveway.

"You see this?" Chuck asks, pointing to the Gadsden flag banner hanging from the gate outside Dave's trailer. Yellow, with a snake coiled tightly. The words "Don't tread on me" across the bottom.

"Yep."

"Well, he's treading on us, ain't he?" Chuck hopes Dave will hear the challenge in his voice but sees nothing on his neighbor's face indicating whether he's reading between the lines.

"Can you believe, Mindy just talked me into buying our place this past year? We been renting for almost a decade. Just talked me into buying. We're shit outta luck now. No park's gonna take our place."

Chuck nods. He thinks this is also true for maybe three-quarters of the park. Maybe more.

"And that bullshit about 'your right to form a Homeowner's association and match the buyer's offer. Shit. None of us could come up with $650,000 if we sold our hair, teeth, and asses." Chuck crosses his arms over his chest.

"Reminds me of the big kid on the playground who holds the little kids' lunch just outta reach and says 'hey, you can get it, no one's stoppin' you," Dave says, his breath is coming out in wisps of smoke now in the cold night air. "What are you planning to do?" he asks.

Chuck pauses before answering.

"I got a few plans in mind. When the time comes."

\* \* \*

### Francis Lot 8

Francis sits on the worn couch. In one hand, a phone number scrawled on paper. Above the phone number, the name he's come to loathe. The one he looked up on Google. Joe Bonvenuto.

He dials it and waits as the phone rings. His heart pounds. Maybe he'll just hang up. Maybe he'll just try to reason with the man. Maybe he'll just…

"Mr. Bonvenuto? My name's Charlie Kriss," Francis lies over the phone, picking a random name that came into his head.

"Speaking," Benvenuto confirms his identity on the phone. Francis continues with another lie.

"I saw in the Saratoga Business Review that you're in the market for waterfront property. I have some land I'm interested in selling you. How soon would you like to meet?"

\* \* \*

## Grafton Lot 9

Mom told me to go to my room. I can hear her and Dad arguing through the walls, anyway. She should have let me stay in the living room so I could watch my show. Darby sits in the bed with me, licking my face because he knows I'm upset. They get loud. Something about the fucking new landlord and now we have to go to a shelter. I hear Dad say Darby's name. He says Darby has to go to a shelter and they'll kill him because he's an old dog.

Darby has good ears. They perked up every time Dad said his name. So, I know he heard Dad and now I lick his face too because I know he's upset.

"Don't worry Darby, I won't let them kill you," I tell him.

Late at night, I put all the dog treats in my backpack. And my wallet with twenty dollars in it from Christmas. And some underwear because you're supposed to change it every day. And some hotdogs. And I wrap Darby in blankets, so he won't get cold. I take him out the door.

I didn't really figure out where we would go. And I forgot to pack enough food. I saw the sign for a free hot breakfast at the church, so I tucked Darby in his blankets under my coat and went inside. It's all grownups and you're supposed to show ID. I don't have any. And I don't want them to know my name. The lady at the door tells me to wait. She points to a chair in the corner, and I sit down. She lets the rest of the grownups in.

Darby wriggles and I pet him, so he'll keep quiet. I count the people coming in. This is boring. They don't have TV. Usually,

I watch TV when I'm bored, or when Mom has to go out, or when I finish my homework, or when I can't sleep.

My feet start to get jittery. When we used to go to school, before lockdown, I got yelled at for jittery feet. It's disruptive. I don't want to be disruptive, so I push my feet down onto the floor to make them stop.

On the wall, there are colorful cards and pamphlets like at the doctor's office. I take one. It has a picture of a cross and a lamb.

It says, "The Lamb of God."

I didn't know God had a farm, but since everything belongs to God, I guess he can have lambs too.

I start reading because the pictures are too boring. It's got a lot of rules about what you should do so you can go to Heaven. Like the stuff Grandma always talks about.

A door opens and a priest comes out, and the woman tells him things quietly. She bothers to be quiet when she doesn't want you to hear something. Not like Mom and Dad, who tell you to go in the other room and yell anyway.

He nods his head, looks at me, and asks me to come with him. I know about priests because Mom's family is Roman Catholic. That means they're Italian. When my dad gets angry, he calls them wops. Mom gets mad when he says this. But then when we go to Burger King Mom orders Whoppers and that's ok.

I go with the priest to an office. I didn't know priests had offices since I only went to Christmas Eve mass a few times with Grandma. But he has an office with papers everywhere and a Jesus statue. I learned about Jesus from Grandma. And about the Commandments. There are ten. They're important, and that's why you say them loud.

Thou Shout not Kill!

Thou Shout not Steal!

Thou Shout not Take Away our Bare Arms!

When it's important, you shout. Like Mom and Dad.

"What's your name, son?" he asks me.

"Can't say."

He nods.

"Why is that?"

"Because you'll make us go back to my parents."

"Us?"

Darby fidgets around and pushes his head out of the top of my coat, and the priest jumps back like he was scared a little, but then he smiles. Darby needs to learn about fidgety feet.

"What's your dog's name, son?"

"Darby," I say before I remember to keep it secret.

"Well, it must be a pretty serious business for you and your dog to come out in the cold looking for some food. I told my assistant to prepare a meal for you, and we'll get something for him, but I really do want to help you get to your family."

"Can't," I tell him.

"Why is that?"

"I heard my mom and dad talking last night. The landlord sold our trailer park. We're going to a shelter. Darby is going to the pound, and they'll kill him for being too old." I try to explain.

He shakes his head. He looks uncomfortable like he doesn't know what to say. So, I try to help him.

"So, Mister, Father…"

"Father Donatello," he says.

"Father Donatello, if you're not supposed to kill, will the people at the pound go to Hell for killing Darby?"

He blinks a few times. He needs more help. I continue.

"If my parents take Darby to the pound, then they go to Hell too, guilt by association, right?" I heard that on a TV show. I know about courts from TV.

"It's not quite like that, exactly."

"If you're not supposed to steal, then the guy who takes our house is a sinner, right? So, he's going to Hell?"

"Jesus wants us to love our enemies. He wants us to forgive those who sometimes do the wrong thing."

"But they can steal our house and kill my dog and I'm supposed to forgive them?"

"Yes. Sort of."

"That's wrong."

The door opens, and a lady walks in with a tray. I see the steam coming off of a plate of French toast, oatmeal. Darby is excited. He smells the food.

I give him my French toast first. No time to eat. I need to get to the bottom of this.

"The new landlord is Italian. I heard Dad say his name. So, he's probably Catholic, right? He knows about sinning, and Hell, and he's ignoring Jesus anyway, isn't he? Is that why Hell happens after you die? So, you can at least get to do what you want for now and pay later? Is it like financing? My mom got financing on the air conditioning. You buy it now and pay later, but they charge you more. It's called interest. Because things get more interesting when you make more money."

Father sits on his hands and bites his lower lip. I don't understand why he's so confused. He's supposed to know all about Jesus.

"I think this is an important time to pray and ask God for guidance. He has a plan. We need to have faith in his plan and show mercy to our fellow man, even when they upset us."

I hold up the pamphlet from the front room. The one with the boring pictures, and I wave it at him.

"But it says here that Jesus said, 'Blessed are the poor, for theirs is the Kingdom of Heaven.' My family's poor. Does Jesus like you better and let you into Heaven when you're poor? He's not really helping us here. Danny Coltrane lives in a big house, but he beats me up and steals my lunch. So, he's going to Hell, but not until he dies. Meanwhile, my family's poor and we're going to lose our house. So maybe Jesus will help me out for a change?"

I ask him questions as Darby cleans the plate that was meant for me. I don't mind. Father Donatello doesn't have very good answers. Did he not do his homework in Jesus school?

"Tell you what, our church has a special fund for families in need. If I promise to help your family find a new home where you wouldn't have to lose your dog, will you tell me your name and let me bring you home to your family?"

I consider this and then agree.

* * *

## Francis Lot 8

Francis sits at the Starbucks in downtown Saratoga, one hand shading the afternoon sunlight pouring in the big storefront windows. The other steadying his laptop. He logs in to their Wi-Fi with the password the barista gave him. Until now he had no use for Facebook. But just the other day, his nephew showed him how to go Live. *Imagine that.*

It didn't even occur to the kid to ask why his Uncle Fran suddenly wanted to become a Facebook... what do the kids call them, influencers? Francis tried to recall. No matter, he looks over the list of instructions.

Just before he cues up his Facebook Livestream, he opens another tab, copies one email address, then another, into his email. News 10, News 13, The Adirondack Tribune. One by one he sends out the same message.

"I've got a story you're going to want to cover. Be first on the scene. Starbucks on Broadway." He adds ten minutes to the time of his meeting with Bonvenuto and hits send.

*I'm all set for my meeting now.*

As he waits for his guest, Francis thinks of the younger man and his wife. Or girlfriend. These days you can't guess. The one who came strolling by that morning. With the long strip of a goatee peeking out from beneath his face mask. What had his name been? Gary? Jerry? Francis should remember the man's name. The man who had been his inspiration. He had been right. No sense going out like a fart in a dust storm. May as well make a statement. Go viral. Like the young people love to do with their videos.

He takes a sip of his coffee. It's foul and overpriced. But he needed to blend in, at least at first. He nurses the drink while glancing out the window to scan the streets downtown. And waits.

\* \* \*

# Jerry

"Jerry! Jerry, get in here," Lois calls out from the living room. Jerry's office is in the back of the house. He hears her call his name, groans under his breath, and continues entering link after link onto the excel spreadsheet. Careful to create content for each day of the month, five slots per day. All to please his newest client.

"Jeeeerrrryyy! You've got to see this!"

He closes his eyes and heaves a sigh before swiveling in his chair and getting up.

*Maybe there's been another insurrection. It's that time of the year.*

He grabs an apple from the fruit basket on the marble countertop as he passes through the kitchen. Lois stands hands on her hips, blocking their large, mounted plasma television.

"That's the guy, isn't it?"

He can now see it. He fingers his Pringle's mustache, twirling the waxed hair into a curl.

Not Washington D.C., but downtown Saratoga Springs. Not a government building, but a familiar storefront. Tall windows framed on the top by a forest green sign, the telltale crowned mermaid, a familiar trademark.

He swallows a piece of apple, watching the screen. A crowd is gathered, local and state police, even a swat team, interspersed with reporters on the scene.

"That's the guy!" Lois yells. Jerry steps in closer. The scene comes into focus. An almost empty storefront, two figures inside. One of them is Fran.

"Holy shit!" Jerry says, dropping the apple.

\* \* \*

## Chuck LOT 15

"Donna! That's him!" Chuck yells, not realizing his wife has dozed in her chair. She startles awake, and it takes a few moments for her to catch her breath.

"Sorry, but you have to see this." Chuck leans close to reassure her and to make sure she's OK. Then he gestures to the screen with the remote control while turning up the volume. He can hardly believe the guy from across the street who helps him shovel out his car in a storm, who rakes everyone's leaves in the fall and bakes tins of lemon frosted cookies for all the neighbors every Christmas time, is now going off at Starbucks. He turns to his wife.

"Look who it is."

\* \* \*

## Jayden LOT 7

"Holy shit!"

Jayden perks up. Her grandmother never swears. Even several rooms away, behind the thick walls at Grandma's house, nothing like the paper-thin walls at her mom's trailer, the startled curse reverberated. A call to arms. Jayden had been slowly walking toward the kitchen for a snack, texting Sophie and not minding her grandmother, who was preoccupied with Fox News in the living room. But now, intrigued, she picks up her pace.

Too late. Her grandmother switches off the TV as Jayden rounds the corner into the ample living room.

"I'm sorry, I shouldn't have sworn. This is not appropriate for you. Take Danny in the guest room and do your homework."

*Whatever. I hate living here. I want my mom to come home from rehab. I want to go back to our place. Unless it's gone already.*

Jayden shepherds her brother into the spare room, letting the door close harder than necessary.

She's beginning to detest the guest room she has to share with her brother, which is gross and annoying.

"What is it?" Danny asks.

"We're gonna watch a movie, but it's a secret." Jayden sits him on the bed and pulls up YouTube on her laptop. She lowers the volume and looks up Fox News. Whatever had made her grandmother swear, it must be good.

She scrolls through a few segments and clicks on the video with the Live tag.

"This is boring!" Danny whines.

"Wait for it…"

She recognizes the scene. The Starbucks on Broadway. And then she recognizes the name.

*"I've accepted an offer from Bonvenuto Real Estate."* She recalls the name from the letter Mom got from the landlord. The letter they got just around Christmas. The news that made Mom relapse.

Jayden also recognizes someone else.

The guy who always had the best candy on Halloween. Who gave Baxter treats when she took him for a walk. The guy who helped her mom get Danny to the doctor when he had the flu and their car wasn't working, even though it cost him a day's work. The guy who chased kids from the bus stop away when they had tried to follow her home, taunting her for being poor.

He looked rough. But it was definitely him.

\* \* \*

### Jerry

Lois is up and pacing, rubbing her hands over her eyes in a theatric soap-opera gesture.

"My God! We're accomplices! We're fucking accomplices!"

"Relax, he did this all on his own." Having thrown out the rest of the apple, Jerry now lifts a glass of sparkling water, as if toasting Francis through the TV screen.

"They're gonna kill him! Or he's gonna kill that guy! Or both!"

Jerry smooths his mustache flat against his upper lip.

"He was going to kill himself anyway. And if what he said is true, that man, Bonvenuto or whatever his name is, is a douche."

"You're nuts! You're completely nuts!" Lois screams.

"Get it! Get it!" He shouts at the screen, lifting the bottle in salutation.

"That's what you say to a man with a gun to his head?"

"That's what I say to one of these rich bastards finally getting what they deserve!"

"But that could be you!"

"We're more likely to be Fran than that douchebag. Nothing wrong with a man taking out the trash." Jerry sips his sparkling water and puts his feet up.

* * *

## Grafton Lot 9

The car is nice and warm. It's fancy, there aren't any soda stains on the dashboard. Father Donatello starts the car and within minutes I want to cry. I reach a hand down under my bottom.

"The seat's warm. But I don't think I peed myself because I'm dry." I tell Father Donatello.

"Oh, no, you're fine. It's a seat warmer. It's part of the car."

It's like a car from a movie. Darby likes it, I can tell. It's so fancy, we could live in it.

At least it would be better than living in a shelter. I think again about Heaven and judgment and how it sounds like court shows on TV. I wonder if he'll have to stand trial when he dies, and who are the witnesses? I'd be a good witness.

"Your honor, it says here in the Bible that if you lie and steal and kill, you go to Hell. The landlord is guilty on all counts! He should be sentenced to life followed by two consecutive Hell sentences!"

The car slows down, but we're not at my home yet. We're downtown, near all the shops. But we can never afford to go to the shops, only to look inside the windows. Dad makes fun of the people who shop here. Mom laughs at his jokes, but I see her looking in the windows sometimes like she really wants to buy the stuff inside. But no one is shopping today. There's people around and news cameras and police. The road ahead is blocked off, a cop is waving the cars ahead to turn in another direction.

"What's all that?" I ask.

"It looks like some kind of emergency, maybe a fire."

Father sounds upset.

"Are they shooting a movie?"

"I don't think so."

If they are shooting a movie, maybe we can get jobs as extras. That's what I heard about in school. They'll pay you to stand there and be in the background. Maybe it's a lot. Maybe I can get my career in acting started that way. If I decide not to become a lawyer. Or a priest.

Father turns down the side street and switches on the radio. I hope it's not country music. It's news talk. He turns up the volume.

"We have an active shooter situation at the Starbucks on Broadway…"

"Was that what that was? A real shooter? Like in the schools?" I ask

"Um, I don't know."

Darby is curious. He stares out the window too. His tail is wagging. He must want to be in the movies too. If it is a movie.

Active shooter, the lady's voice on the radio said.

"Don't worry," I tell Father, "We have active shooter drills at school all the time. You follow the instructions and sit under your desk until the teachers say it's over. It's just like a fire drill, except you don't line up and go outside."

But when we do the drills, it's practice. They don't shut down the streets outside.

\* \* \*

## Francis Lot 8

*Well, here we are. Only one of us is getting out of this alive.* Fran has a split second to back out. He considers changing his mind. He could excuse himself and head to the bathroom and then take a detour and exit the building. Instead, he tracks Bonvenuto as the businessman walks through the door, puts in his order, and scans the tables. Francis feels his right-hand wave in a greeting, gesturing him forward. He could back out now, but instead, he waits for Bonvenuto to remove his coat and sit opposite him at the table.

As Bonvenuto greets him, Fran pulls the gun from his laptop bag and stands up, holding the weapon in both sweaty hands, sweeping it from side to side. The chatter dies down. A woman screams.

"Shut up!" Fran yells.

They do.

His heart is pounding now. He motions with the gun in the direction of the door and mouths the words "Get out!" afraid that if he speaks his voice will crack. They flee for the exit. Customers, baristas, all of them. Who is gonna argue with a gun?

And now it's just Bonvenuto. He starts whimpering in the same annoying key as the piped-in elevator music. A crowd starts to gather outside. A man hastily sets up his tripod with a camera marked with the number 10. Let them see. Let them all see.

He turns back to Bonvenuto. He's whimpering and drool is spilling over his mouth. Disgusting. Fran turns over his shoulder to grab some napkins from the counter. Instead, he sees a steaming hot cup of coffee with the name 'Joe' scrawled across it in black marker. He grabs the drink and waves it in Bonvenuto's face.

"This yours, *Joe?* Look at you! Throwing your money away on this overpriced shit!"

Fran throws the drink across the room. It hits the wall and coffee splatters but he's not paying attention. His eyes are fixed on Bonvenuto.

"Ya know," he begins, voice steady but menacing, "maybe if you cut back on lattes, you wouldn't need a fifth boat storage unit. Ya know? If you would just," he slams a hand on the table for emphasis, "learn," slam, "to live," slam, "within your means," slam. "Then you wouldn't need to make decent people homeless."

Fran tightens his grip on the gun, aiming again at Bonvenuto's head. He thinks he hears a siren in three-part harmony now with Bonvenuto's whimpering and the ambient music. *Girl from Ipanema.* He won't have much time. Fran grabs the duct tape from his laptop bag and checks his laptop again. Yes, baby, we are live!

Bonvenuto heaves frantic breaths as Fran wraps the tape around him and secures him to his chair.

"What are your last words before I send you straight to Hell?"

He starts crying for real now.

"What do you want from me?"

"Isn't it obvious?"

Fran grabs the back of the chair and drags him to the doorway, swinging his hand- the one with the gun- to indicate to the people outside to stand back and clear the way.

He opens the door and heaves Bonvenuto out onto the top step, then ducks down behind him. Just to buy time, there's no escaping this alive.

"I'm calling a press conference," Fran announces. He tries not to look at the armed police, all training their guns on him.

*Just as well. But I'm not done yet.*

"I want the press up front! Now!" Fran jabs the gun toward Bonvenuto's head, his own head close enough that he can duck behind his captive. He won't escape alive, he knows, but for now, Bonvenuto is his shield. For now, he can be useful for something.

Most of the press remains in the background but a few make their way to the front as instructed.

"Write this down! I got a headline for you! Write it down! Businessman wipes out housing to build boat storage!"

They're recording and some are writing frantically on notepads. "Now make sure your cameras are rolling, you're gonna want to get all of this."

And they do.

"This fucker's making me homeless! Should I kill him? What d'ya think?"

Silence at first, but to Fran's surprise, a slow applause begins in the back of the crowd. He can't be certain, but he thinks he just heard someone yell "off with his head!"

Fran notices one of the reporters upfront, he's kneeling on the sidewalk, has a perfect view. Got his phone up. Fran realizes his laptop, live streaming inside, is missing the best part. "You!" Fran calls out to him, "You, you live streaming this?" He nods his head.

Fran's voice steadies as he calls out to an invisible audience of online fans. "If you're watching this, give a 'like' if you're tired of greedy bastards taking your air. Go on, vote with your thumbs!"

\* \* \*

## Jayden Lot 7

There's a thump on the guest room door. "Danny, let Baxter in." Jayden doesn't take her eyes from her laptop. Keeping the video of the breaking news on one tab, she opens another and types the phrase "class traitor" into Google.

Danny opens the door and Baxter bounds into the room and jumps on the bed. Danny sits beside the dog, staring at the glowing screen as if by habit. Jayden pays him no mind.

She reads the definition, still not sure what her mother meant. Or what it has to do with losing their home. She switches tabs and is back to the Livestream.

She doesn't understand what a class traitor is, but she understands who this guy is, tied up in the chair. He just made his intentions clear. Under the gun, so to speak. But he said it.

"If you're watching this, give a 'like' if you're tired of greedy bastards taking your air..." the guy with the gun just said. Francis. From across the street. Jayden opens Facebook in a new tab.

"Wait! It was just starting to get good!" Danny complains.

"Hold on, it's about to get better," Jayden reassures him. She finds the video livestreaming. She clicks the thumbs up. Then she finds it on Insta and does the same. She does this again and again; on every platform she can find.

She thinks of Mom in rehab. How she almost died, again. How she was doing so much better. She sees the man in the chair. She keeps voting.

\* \* \*

## Jerry

"Wow! Can you believe this guy? How Francis got his groove back." His eyes are now glued to the TV Jerry's leaning off the very edge of the couch. Lois makes a sound of disgust and gets up to leave the room.

"You shouldn't cheer him on!"

"Why not? You know what this rich bastard was going to do. He's just being taught a lesson is all."

\* \* \*

## Grafton Lot 9

I cover Darby's ears as Father Donatello pulls the car over. Darby is shivering. There was gunfire on the radio, and it scared him. Father Donatello opens the door. Probably to go get the dead guy. Priests are always there when people die. It's part of their job. But he doesn't go get the dead guy. He stumbles out of the car and pukes in a snowbank. Maybe he's scared too.

I don't know why. We watch people getting shot on TV all the time. But some people aren't allowed to watch those shows, like my friend Brandon. He's not allowed to watch any violent shows. So maybe Father Donatello wasn't allowed to either and he can't handle it.

Sometimes, when I get scared, I try to figure things out. So, I try to help Father Donatello figure this out, so he won't be scared.

"So, that cop killed that guy. So now he's a sinner, right? So, he'll go to Hell?"

Father looks like he's gonna be sick again. "It's not exactly like that."

"But if the crazy guy had shot the guy in the chair, he would go to jail, right? And then to Hell. So, the cop, is he going to go to jail at least?"

"I think this is a good time to pray for the departed."

"Too late for that. He's already dead. If you were going to help him, why didn't you do it while he was alive?"

\* \* \*

## Chuck Lot 15

The trailer feels colder than usual. Quieter, as Chuck turns off the news. It's over.

He shakes his head and walks into the kitchen, busying himself washing dishes. When all is said and done, he still won. Francis is dead. Of course. Game over. He thinks about the supplies in the shed. Would he still go through with it? What difference would it make?

Later that night, he tucks Donna in and settles into bed beside her.

He closes his eyes and tries to think of justice.

He hears the ticking sound from the cowbell. The sound meant to emulate a clock.

Even with eyes closed, he sees the footage from the news. Fran, out of his mind.

*Could have been me.*

That greedy bastard. Tied to a chair. These images superimposed on the vision of what he had been planning. He imagines his car. Rigged with explosives. Speakers blaring. Singing.

*Cuckoo.*

About how time has come.

He imagines the explosion.

Fantasizes about the looks of horror. To lose their boats. Their precious storage unit.

But it's just a dream.

*I have no home.*

# CLASS REUNION

Marci pulls at the dress. It's been years since she bought it for the kind of party she doesn't get invited to anymore. It doesn't fit. A few years in survival mode will do that.

It will have to do.

She gives it another tug into place and stares in the mirror at the bags under her puffy eyes. Behind her, someone flushes a toilet. She searches her bag for Chapstick while a woman she doesn't recognize emerges from the stall and washes her hands.

The stranger's perfume is light and flowery. She runs her slender hands under the faucet. She's got a 5 a.m. Spin-Class body and Marci thinks she's probably had a few kids and hidden the evidence thanks to Beach Body and a personal trainer. Her dress is slinky, black, and trendy. The stranger doesn't bother to talk to Marci. Then again, Marci doesn't bother to talk to her either.

The stranger shakes her hands dry over the sink and Marci notices a chunky, sparkling diamond wedding ring on the finger of her left hand. The sight makes Marci cringe, imagining the stranger accidentally stabbing herself in the eyeball with such a rock.

It's opulent. Gaudy. Unnecessary. The stranger carefully touches up her makeup as if she's the only one in the room.

It's like High School all over again.

Marci leaves the restroom and heads back out to the ballroom where the floor vibrates to the 90s playlist. Designed to help enhance our journey down memory lane.

It was a mistake to come here.

She tries to fake a smile and wonders if her plastered on happy face is fooling anyone. As she walks through the crowd, Marci greets people she barely remembers. There were two people she hoped to see. One canceled last minute. Boss called him into work. Like Marci, he's low on the pecking order.

She doesn't want to think that it's been twenty years since she's seen these people. Twenty years since she could recall their names. Since their names mattered. Dictating by proximity who held status and who didn't.

Most of them moved away, including the few she had been close friends with. Marci had gotten buried with work. Then more work. And more. Suddenly years were swallowed up in eight hours, five days, then six, then seven. She had lost touch.

"Marci!" a voice distracts her from fidgeting with the ill-fitting dress.

"Cheryl!" They hug. Ok, that was a win, Marci thinks, she always liked her.

"Meet my husband, Tom," she pushes the man by her side forward. They shake hands. Marci thinks he looks like most of the other guys here. Same early signs of baldness buzzed close to make it look like a choice and not a force of nature. Same beard. Same suit.

"So, what are you doing these days?"

Laid off isn't a good look, so she's been using the term "entrepreneur" to make her numerous gig jobs sound less failure-y.

"Oh," Cheryl looks encouraging but confused, smiling, and nodding her head. "Well, I'm a professor at my Alma Mater, teaching English Literature. Love Academia, and Tom here is VP of his company's IT department. We're living in Saratoga now, just bought a house after we sold our last house. Our new place is the perfect size for our family. Two kids!" She gestures with two fingers to drive home how fecund and successful they've been.

Marci sips her soda and nods.

"How about you? Where are you living now? Do you have any kids?"

"No, no kids, my partner and I are, uh, we're doing kind of a minimalist thing." She nods as the words come out. It's a sexy way to describe living in your car.

"Oh! Love it! Like Marie Kondo?"

More like Ted Kaczynski, Marci thinks, but she just smiles and nods. "Yes, exactly." She looks around now for someone else to give her a reason to end this conversation. No luck.

"So, what's your guy do?"

"Oh, well, he's uh, he's on disability."

She makes a weird squinting smiley face at this. "Oh, like in a wheelchair?"

"Not exactly."

"Oh, well, uh, well it was nice seeing you!" she says with the enthusiasm Marci imagines she would have if a child threw up on her shoe and she was trying to be polite.

Marci tries not to hold it against Cheryl. She's grown accustomed to this reaction. If they had a penny for everyone who proclaimed "but, he doesn't look disabled!" they could buy a mansion.

In the background, the 90s pop music continues to blast through the speakers. It's almost as unbearable as the conversations. Marci wonders what she had been expecting. She shouldn't have come. The same popular kids with their parents' wealth to give them a boost are the same picture-perfect adults, posing for selfies together.

They've got their skeletons too. A miscarriage, infidelity, and carefully shrouded nervous breakdown among the lot of them. But they have the safety net to pass it off. To bounce back. To show up twenty years later and compare notes. Any hill they ever had to climb was more gently sloped than the rest of us.

"Hey, Marci!" She turns and sees a man holding a tray. How does he know my name?

"It's Jason. From homeroom."

And now she recognizes him. Even senior year he had been skinny and clean shaven. Now, he sports facial hair over a full face. She never would have recognized him on her own but is relieved he spoke up.

They hug. "Oh my God, thank goodness you're here! I was starting to think it was a mistake to blow all that money on a ticket!"

He laughs. "Well, I'm not exactly here as a guest."

She looks more closely and realizes he's wearing a uniform. "Well, you got the better part of the deal, all things considered. The tickets were way overpriced."

He agrees.

"How are you doing? What are you up to?"

"Well," he begins, "I lost my job in 2008, company closed down, and since I didn't finish college- Mom got sick- I ended up driving Uber, DJ'ing, and waiting tables. It's enough to split an apartment with two other dudes and still kinda get by, so you know."

"I hear you. You're not alone. We just lost our place last month. Although I managed to outlast 2008, we got downsized in 2014. Couldn't pay the student debts and mortgage on one income, especially after my partner had to go on disability."

"Yeah, that sucks."

Marci nods. They look around at the others. The privileged. Neither Marci nor Jason needs to say it. They were no more deserving. We were no less deserving. And yet here we are.

"Well, maybe we can catch up for drinks sometime when it's less, uh, nineties out?" he says.

"Agreed."

She watches him disappear into a back room. Asking herself again, *why did I bother to come?* They had graduated two decades ago, and yet everyone stayed in their caste.

In their own lanes.

*Did I need to pay money to be reminded of this?*

# MIDDLE MANAGER

"Does it always take five hours?" I ask the clerk behind the desk. Bill, his nametag indicates, doesn't seem to be in a chatty mood. According to his nametag, he's the assistant manager.

Middle management at the Department of Social Services can't be a fun gig. But eye contact would be nice.

"Hello?" I ask again, just to make sure he hasn't fallen asleep. Or had a stroke.

Bill looks up. He blinks a few times and looks like I've interrupted something important. As if flipping through stacks of papers is his life support and my presence here has interfered.

"Hmmm?" he asks.

"Just saying hello, is all. I'm Denise. I'm filing for benefits."

He shuffles papers for another few minutes before rapid-firing questions. Not expecting a word from him, I startle.

"Recent place of employment?"

"Buster's Bakery."

"Never heard of it."

"Well, it's too late now. They're closed. Look I need to know how much financial assistance I can get and how soon. My landlord's threatening to kick me out and I just got done paying off my car before the pandemic and the store had to close and …"

Eyes still on his stack of paper, he points to a sign on the cubicle behind him.

*Lack of planning on your part doesn't constitute an emergency on mine...*

"Um, ok. Well, I'm pretty sure lack of planning had nothing to do with this. I mean, did you plan on the pandemic?"

"We're not here to talk about me," Bill remarks, he stares at me as if I've just shit on his laptop.

"I just spent five hours here, so I was just trying to get some answers is all." I try to explain. He doesn't seem to care.

* * *

"Bill, I need to see you in my office," John's call wasn't expected. Probably a complaint from some agitated client who didn't get a letter on time because they didn't have all of their paperwork completed.

Lack of planning, I always tell them.

And now it's my mess to clean up.

I close my tabs on the computer and forward my calls to voicemail.

"Good morning, Gina," I pass by my colleague whose eyes are on her phone.

"Hey, Bill," she barely notices me as she answers.

I knock on John's door.

"Come in!"

I close the door behind me. He points to the chair across the desk from him. It's old. The cushion is torn. But this is social services. No big corner office here, not even for the director.

"What's up?"

He closes a tab on his computer and turns back to me.

"I'm sure you know from watching the news that the county is hurting. Because of the lockdowns and all. We're operating far outside of our budget."

"Yes, I imagine so."

"Well, we're going to have to make some cuts. No way around it."

"Desperate times call for desperate measures, they say."

"Well, I'm glad you think so. Your position is being terminated."

My throat dries up.

"What? Me? But I'm an assistant supervisor. Who else will do my job?"

"Well, we've hired a consulting firm to help with restructuring and it's been determined that the role of assistant supervisor is redundant. You have two weeks."

Two weeks. After fifteen years with the department.

"But my wife got laid off because of the shutdowns. Our oldest is going to start college next week. I just took out a new loan to cover repairs. I can't afford to lose my income. It will take weeks for unemployment to come in."

"Bill," he begins, folding his arms over his chest, "lack of planning on your part does not constitute an emergency on mine."

# A Most Horrible Site

**The following is a work of fiction, in the genre of horror.**

**Unless it is a work of true crime, in the genre of capitalism.**

A most horrible sight. The kind to make most pull a u-turn and drive away.

Not wanting to live too close to a place like this.

*Can you imagine what it looks like on the inside?* They whisper. And never

*Can you imagine trying to survive all this time?*

Only

*What's wrong with people who live like this?*

Never

*What's wrong with people who allow their neighbors to fall?*

Walled apart by broken furniture, rusted cars, windows taped in plastic.

A most horrible sight, the holes in the roof with no able body to fix them. Gaps in the walls with no livable wage to make ends meet.

And that's only the view from outside. Door closed. A pile of rubble obscures the view of the inside.

*My treasures*, she calls them.

The things he left behind.
The things she won't dare part with.
Because she'll need them someday.
And there may not be money to replace what's lost.
*Once you've got it, keep it.*
As the treasures mount, blocking out the sun.
Casting shadows in the dark.
A most horrible sight, the remnants of decades of trickle-down disappointment.

A most horrible sight. A stranger pulling in, looking side to side over his shoulder. Not wanting to spend one moment more than necessary.
Only time to exit the truck and nail his notice to the door.
Of this most horrible site.
Now void of life.
A graveyard lined with plastic tombs. Old bicycles and coolers. A grill and chairs.
A collection of broken mementos.
An offering made in hopes of better times returning.
The Vesuvius of the working poor.
One of many he'll remember. Entertaining his family at dinner later. With tales of the grotesque places he's condemned.
And as they shake their heads and chuckle, he'll point a finger at his son and say, "do your homework so you can get a good job and not end up like that."
And never
"Tear down the patriarchy so a widowed woman doesn't end up condemned to live like that."

And never

"Agitate for universal healthcare so an elderly woman never needs to end up like that."

And never

"Fight for a livable wage so no one ever ends up living like that."

And never

Thinks twice about how close he is to ending up like that.


*A most horrible sight*, they said. The last straw. They tried everything else, but nothing worked. An intervention was needed.

And never a safety net.

An intervention.

And never a guaranteed income.

An intervention.

And never socialism.

Only regulations, citations, another case to manage.

What they found in the bedroom was a bridge too far.

"Poor dog was frozen to death." They said.

And never

*How could we have kept the heat on?*

And never

*How could we?*

Only

*How could she?*


A most horrible sight, I see.

Superimposed on the warm body on my lap.

Who breathes in time with me.

As I worry about where we'll live next.
Who licks my hand.
As I try to work one more hour to stay ahead.
With the image in my mind.
Of the most horrible sight, that could be us.

# Good Liberal White Woman

"Karen, I love your new yoga pants!" Lori tells me as she walks into the studio. She always gets here before me because her office is close by.

I rush in to place my mat on the floor beside Lori. Despite my asking, she always forgets to save a spot for me, but I manage to squeeze in next to her before anyone claims that space in the studio.

The air is scented with some blend of incense. I try to sniff discreetly, dissecting the aroma, with no luck. All I know is, the blend is already setting my mind at ease.

"Ladies, a gentle reminder that we are wearing masks now in the studio," Laxmi, our yoga instructor, chimes in. She's about four feet tall and ninety pounds soaking wet and her long blond hair looks recently highlighted. She wears a purple mask with the Om symbol on it.

I smile and nod, securing my mask over my mouth but letting my nose peak out. I have to be able to breathe, after all.

"Thank you," I tell Laxmi, otherwise ignoring our much younger instructor. She has a lot to learn about the world, and as someone who is her senior by at least two decades, I sometimes find it difficult to take her instruction seriously.

"Can you believe she's giving in to all this fear-based nonsense?" I ask Lori when Laxmi is out of earshot. Lori rolls her eyes.

I pull down my mask to drink out of my water bottle. Fifteen minutes to the start of class. I've been able to do my job managing the bank's HR from home, so arriving early to make it before the limited cut off hasn't been too hard. Especially if I work through my lunch break. Not as early as Lori, but I'm not one of these rude people who rush in at the last minute.

I notice Lori's mask and what appears to be a black and white lotus, but when my eyes adjust, I realize it's a fist. "What is that?" I ask her.

"It's to show my support for Black Lives Matter. A lady at work was selling these. The money is going to establish a sensitivity-training library at the office, so we can buy books to teach ourselves how to be anti-racist."

"I think that's a great idea, I fully support civil rights and we always give the kids' old books and clothes to inner-city charities. I just wish they wouldn't resort to vandalism. I mean, being destructive is no way to get your point across. No one listens to you when you're disrespectful."

"Well, according to the books I've been reading, many Black people don't feel like they have a platform since white people haven't historically listened to their interests."

"You can make those excuses now," I tell Lori, "you're young and you rent. But when you get into your own home, mark my words, you're going to feel very differently about property damage. How would you like it if you work hard to pull yourself up by your bootstraps only to have an angry mob come and break the windows in your house or business?"

"I read online that a lot of the damage was by outside agitators," Lori responds. I don't like her tone. I come to yoga to relax, not to worry about someone vandalizing my home.

"You just aren't appreciating the progress we've made. This is the problem with you young liberals. You make the perfect the enemy of the good. Take the slogan 'defund the police,' for example. Now, if we didn't have police, who would you call when someone tries to rob or rape you?"

"Police don't prevent crime. They show up after the fact. Besides, defunding the police just means putting the money into social services."

"I'm starting to think that library you're paying for is filling your mind with nonsense. I mean, it's just common sense. Last weekend, for my birthday, Fred wanted to take me out to a nice dinner, and we got stuck for an hour here on Broadway because of protestors marching through the streets. What do they think they're going to accomplish? All they were doing was making a scene and making people uncomfortable."

"Maybe it's time people were made uncomfortable," Lori says, and it's like she's trying to push my buttons.

"Well, suit yourself. I prefer to support peaceful causes. Like charities that help essential workers. Look how they're being neglected! A lot of them are People of Color."

"Ok, class, we're going to get started," Laxmi announces.

Thank God for small favors.

Just as she's dimming the lights, a young Black woman rushes in, yoga mat in hand. "I'm sorry, I couldn't get out of work early, can I just squeeze in?"

Laxmi looks around the room. I follow her gaze. Patricia, in the back, is retired. She's been waiting an hour. Lillian is a stay-at-home mom and pretends she hasn't heard the commotion. Melissa is an executive. She donates a lot to the studio, rumor has it, so I can understand why Laxmi doesn't so much as make eye contact with her. She looks anxious as she waits for one of us to voluntarily give up our spot.

I side-eye Lori. Lori looks back at me. She doesn't say anything at first. I notice she tries to face the front of the class, away from the door, but after a few moments, she looks to the back of the room. The young woman sees her. Still, she remains silent.

"I'm terribly sorry, but if no one is willing to give up their spot for this class, I'm afraid we're full. Maybe try to come earlier next time?" Laxmi offers weakly.

The woman turns away and leaves.

\* \* \*

I feel guilty for a moment. But my life is stressful, and self-care is essential to a spiritual lifestyle. I really need this class. And it was worth all the angst. As awful as the class started, I must say it was one of the better classes I've had with Laxmi. But I guess it's like they say, sometimes you have to sit with discomfort to clear your aura and truly heal.

As the class disperses, I stroll over to Starbucks to grab a Nitro Cold Brew with Cinnamon and Oatmilk Foam, my favorite. The line isn't too long, thank God. But the kid behind the counter is slow as molasses and of course, when it's my turn, I can tell this is going to be a problem.

"Ma'am, we require you to wear a mask while in the store," she tells me.

The attitude of some people.

"Masks don't work anyway and according to my doctor, wearing a mask will trigger my asthma, so this is how I wear it. So, deal with it."

I put in my order, and it takes forever to arrive. One sip and I can tell something is wrong with it.

"Excuse me, this is not what I ordered."

"Ma'am, you have to put your mask back on," she tells me.

"I am a grown woman with a college degree, do not talk to me like that! I'm telling you this is not what I ordered, and I demand to speak to the manager!" I'm screaming now and I don't care. Whatever happened to customer service?

She rolls her eyes at me and that's the last straw.

"You want to disrespect your customers? See where you'll get in life! No wonder this job is the best you can do! You won't have this job for long after I complain to corporate!"

You know what happened? The manager came out from the back. Asked me to leave the store. I slammed the door on the way out and cracked the window. I'm going to file a complaint directly to the corporate office. Some people just don't know how to act.

# TWIST OF FATE

**Fate:** *the development of events beyond a person's control, regarded as determined by a supernatural power.*

It couldn't be helped.

Being defined this way.

How fortunate for that lucky man, and you know it was a man, who just happened to have the job of deciding the meanings of words.

How fortunate that God is dead, unless a tree limb crushes your roof, an act of God. Just ask your insurance agent.

How lucky, you've paid your tithe to the fickle Gods of Insurance.

Pass the hat.

Fate can be twisted.

How lucky are we to live in the age of plastic, invented just in the nick of time?

Time, not so lucky, can be nicked. An accident while shaving a few seconds off your life here, a few minutes here. As we work away the hours. Unyielding. Inflexible.

Unlike Fate, which is curved; a wheel.

Most fortunate.

A twist of Fate that brought the wagon, ridden by the lucky,
pulled by those whose luck had run out.
Fortuna decides, with her cataract eyes, it's all up to chance
From wagons to Cadillacs
*Now you're free to see the world.*
After work.
True believers line up like clockwork.
To make sure the trains run on time
And those not crushed under the wheel
Pick themselves up by grateful bootstraps
Dreaming of their own Fortune someday.
Fate only exists for the poor.
The wealthy spin yarns of being self-made
While the rest line up for lottery tickets
And draft cards.

Fortunate, how capitalism was designed that way.

Twists of Fate
    Close the gates
    For those who are one accident
    Heart attack
    Broken ankle (twisted, it was Fate)
    Pregnancy
    Or bad case of flu
    From the unemployment line.
    Was it predetermined? A Pre-existing condition? Was this
all Foretold? Or was it Foreclosed?

Proponents of Laissez-Faires economics
   Helped along by the Hands of Fate
   Just happen to be in the right place at the right time
   (How Fortunate!)
   Boarding school
   Country club
   Yacht Club
   Golf Course
   Networking Meeting
   Conference
   University
   Gala
   To receive their lucky break.


Luck, as a device, relieves the wealthy of guilt
   Just as Hell, as a device, relieves the victimized of the urge to
seek justice.


The poor live in Hell; yet are taught to chase luck.
   *Hey, you never know.*
   While the wealthy build towers on the backs of those they
call
   Less fortunate.


"It was meant to be!" alternates with "I worked for everything
I have."
   Luck is the privilege of pretending neither statement is false.
   How Fortunate to believe in fairy tales.

If Luck is a Lady, there is dirt under her nails

    Her back is stooped, and fingers gnarled.

    Her spine is bent (a Twist of Fate) from the load she bears.

    Her mind crushed by despair the toll she pays for the salary she earns for the Fortune she makes

    For someone else.

# BREAD AND CIRCUSES

Bread and Circuses
   The Standard American Diet consists of Carbs and cruelty:
for your entertainment.


Modeling, psychologists call it- when a baby smiles at an adult
and expects a smile in return, a frown for a frown.


So, too, does the patronizing patriarchal patricians of industry
model us in their image and convince us it was our own idea.
   We shout into the abyss
   About injustice and indignation
   And the abyss shouts back; an empty echo
   Before we realize we've surrendered revolution for entertain-
ment.


A smile for a smile
   A frown for a frown
   An eye for an eye


They let us believe that art mimics life.
   When in truth they've hijacked art and hypnotized

Read *1984* and *Brave New World*, scream along with Howard Beale, that you can't take it anymore.

Even the kids can play along as David beats Goliath on *A Bug's Life*

Just don't try it in real life.

Mimics art. Mimics strife. Models movements.

Until the line between fantasy and reality is blurred and the suffering of soap stars garners more empathy than the suffering of our brothers and sisters in reality.

We cheer for the underdog in dystopian fantasies
And confuse Wrestlemania pageants of power plays
For righteous anger.
Aiming rage at a caricature
Sucked into the spectacle
Crossing the line into deplorable
Entertained by the loudest and most perverse
The next step in our devolution could only have been
A showman promising to drain the swamp
And make reality entertaining again
Just like in the movies.

We pay the price
For the comfort of fiction
For Jimmy Stewart to rally the people and put Mr. Potter in his place
For Randy Quaid to kick the boss when he shorts Clark a raise
For the underdog to achieve an eleventh-hour win
Showing that justice prevails

And before the credits roll, Pottersville has already been built
Right outside your front door.
And you haven't had a raise in eight years but that's ok
Because your friend gave you his Netflix password
So, you can stop screaming
Into a megaphone
And keep streaming
*Schitt's Creek*
From the comfort of home
and see the wealthy get what they deserve
on-screen.
Never mind, that Goliath crushed David and Howard Beale
is dead
Sedated by the circus while they poison your bread.

# GENERATIONAL WEALTH

"Won't you come in, Steve?" I close the door behind him as he scoots into the living room. I notice he bumped his knee on my bookcase, but then it's not my fault the room is so tiny.

And I've lived here a long time. Long enough to collect a few things.

I gesture to the couch. His eyes sweep the cushions briefly before he sits down. Something his father never would have done.

"I sure do miss the days when your father used to come by to check on things. I'd make him tea and he'd spend a whole afternoon talking with old Betty sometimes. He was a good man."

Steve smiles. I hope he doesn't play poker, not a friendly smile. It's the kind of smile you make when you're about to tell someone you're sleeping with their spouse, but you don't want them to be mad because after all, you're all good friends.

In other words, the reason for his visit is bad news. I gather that much. He eyes my furniture like he's afraid it will come to life and bite him. Or maybe he assumes something is going to crawl out from the cushions. That's what happens when people think poor equals dirty.

"Can I get you any tea?" I ask him.

"Oh, no thank you, Miss, uh," he looks at his clipboard. I know he's pretending he's not looking. He tries to make it seem natural. In spite of himself, he stumbles on my name. The way the doctor down at the clinic stumbles. Can't blame him. They've got a new PA every time I go. Probably got a hundred patients to remember.

Of course, Steve's father knew my name. Knew the names of everyone in the building. He was a good landlord.

Steve stammers for a minute about how he's making the rounds, got a lot of doors to knock on, and can't stay long.

"You know, I remember you when you were just learning to walk," I tell him. He looks surprised.

"Oh, of course, you don't remember, but your father brought you here as a little boy when he had to come and fix things or bring paperwork. And I would give you cookies. That was when my Fred was alive of course. And back then we had a dog named Oscar. You used to love toddling around after Oscar. But that was goodness, a long time ago. It's a different world now I suppose."

I see his face, no longer freckled like back in the day, turn slightly red. Oh, now I've embarrassed him. It's the truth. And you can expect old people to remember young people more than in reverse. We get excited about the young people and whatnot. But what are we to them?

"I hope it's not any trouble. Your father was such a great man and I sure hope you and your family are doing well since his passing, God rest his soul."

"Oh, yeah. Thank you. We are." He sighs heavily and flips open a notebook. "It says here that your lease is annual. So, it's up for renewal in six months."

"Oh, sure. Your father was always good about renewing and I never minded if he was a few months late providing the new lease, we both knew we could count on each other and old Betty ain't going anywhere."

His face turns whiter if you can imagine. Looks like his stomach don't agree with him suddenly. I wonder what I said wrong. I don't have to wonder for too long.

"Well, um, you see," he begins, "with my dad's passing and all, as you know, I inherited his properties."

"Oh, yes, I know he has a few places, this being his first. I was one of his first tenants. Did you know?"

"Uh, I did not," he looks like he's swallowing a fish oil capsule. All bitter and fishy and liable to make you get heartburn on the way down.

"Are you sure you don't need some water?" I ask him.

"No, thank you. So, the reason I am stopping by is to let everyone know, to let you know,"

He stalls and I nod my head, trying to coax it out of him. When you get to be my age suspense is no fun, more like a hindrance that takes up the few minutes you may have left before the Good Lord takes you to your rewards.

"I've been given an offer on the property, and I've accepted."

"Oh, well, congratulations! So, who is the new landlord?"

"Well, there isn't exactly going to be one." He swallows hard and I can tell he hasn't gotten much practice delivering the news.

"What do you mean?"

"It's being sold to a development company. From Texas. They're going to demolish the building and create luxury condos."

He hands me some paperwork and I put it on the table, not breaking eye contact.

"How could you do that? This is my home. Our home."

"Well, technically it isn't. I mean you're just renting. Besides, the buyer is going to give everyone a payout of $1000.00."

"That won't cover moving expenses and all. I don't drive. Neither do half the people in this building."

I start to sound angrier than I intended.

"It's just business. Nothing personal."

I shake my head. "Well, I guess we wasted the money paying for your college because it don't seem like you've learned a whole lot."

"What?"

"Your father always used to say that the rent from this property was your college fund. My rent paid for your education. We," I gesture toward the hallway, indicating the other tenants, "we paid for your degree. So, you could have options as a professional that most of us in this building could never dream of having for ourselves. And this is how you repay us."

He looks away. I can tell he's stumped. His silence is worse than any excuse he could have offered.

"Well, I can tell you one thing. Your father knew better than to treat people this way. He knew some things were more important than making a buck. All the education in the world, and you don't know not to bite the hand that fed you all these years."

# Cost of Living: A Play in Five Acts

**Narrator:**

If we don't participate in the race to the bottom, wage-wise, we will be effectively locked out of the labor market. If we do participate in the wage race to the bottom, we are complicit in cheapening our industries and undercutting our fellow workers.

## Act I

**boss:** here is a job.

**worker:** here is the wage I require in order to live.

**boss:** that is not the wage I will pay you, take the job or I will give it to someone else and you can go to the back of the line.

*\*worker takes a job and then has to take two or three additional jobs to cobble together one poverty-wage\**

## ACT II

**worker:** the equipment you've given me to do the job you've hired me to do is not working.

**boss:** Ok. here is a tool that will work. Now pay for it.

**worker:** I can't afford this tool at the rate you are paying me. I will acquire this tool if you adjust my wages to accommodate the purchase of a tool you are requiring me to use to do the job you have asked me to do at a wage that is already below what I need.

**boss:** I will not buy the tool and if you do not complete the work as I have asked including the use of the tool I demand you use, you can go to the back of the line and look for other work.

*worker buys tool to maintain employment*

## Act III

**class traitor:** I'm selling the place you live, but don't worry, you'll have other options.

**worker:** but I can't afford the other options with my three low-wage jobs and need to pay out of pocket for expenses required of me to do said jobs.

**class traitor:**

**worker:** didn't you say you were going to retire here?

## Act IV

**life insurance agent:** good news! your policy is worth 100,000 dollars.

**worker:** can I get any of that money now?

**life insurance agent:** only if you pay five times more per month to convert to a whole life policy and wait about five years. Lots of people are doing this as an investment strategy, let's sign you up.

**worker:** but I can't afford that because I have to work three jobs and pay for the tools I am required to use to do complete the work and will have to pay to move and pay a higher rent because houses are only for people who can't afford rentals.

**life insurance agent:**

\*\*\*o\*\*\*

## Act V

**class traitor with a badge:** you're not supposed to be on this sidewalk, the sign reads, 'no loitering!"

**worker:** I have no place else to go.

**class traitor with a badge:** go home.

**worker:** this is my home.

**class traitor with a badge:** get a job then.

**worker:** I had three jobs. I couldn't afford to keep them.

### The End

# HEALTHY MART

"Excuse me," I ask the woman kneeling on the floor, putting price stickers on boxes of bamboo-based floss and organic hemp-based kinds of toothpaste. She pulls herself up and brushes off her knees. In the narrow aisle, people walk around us, politely lost in their own worlds.

"Yes? What can I do for you?" she asks as she dodges out of the path of an oncoming shopper who came close to bumping her with his elbow.

I hold up the item in question.

"Can you tell me if this cinnamon and mint clove charcoal-infused organic toothpaste is any good? Like, what does it taste like?"

She laughs, "Oh, I'm sorry miss, I don't actually shop here. I get the Sparkling Clean brand over at Afford-i-Mart."

My eyes widen. I throw up in the back of my mouth a little.

"Really? But you work here. At Healthy Mart, and you don't even buy the products? That's not good for business."

"Well," she says, "maybe not, but if they expect me to buy my groceries here and still have money to pay my bills, they need to pay me more than seven bucks an hour."

"But don't you believe in the company's mission of organic, clean, sustainable living?"

"Oh, sure. But I can't be about sustainable living if I'm dead out in a snowbank because I froze to death because I couldn't pay my rent."

* * *

I can't believe it. I put my basket down right there in the aisle and leave. By the time I've driven my Prius home, I've already made three phone calls, with my blue tooth of course.

I pull up my Mac and do the best thing I can think to do when a grave injustice has taken place. I log in to Facebook.

Status update: I'm shocked to discover that @HealthyMart employs people who do NOT back the Healthy Mart mission! I asked an employee today for a personal recommendation of the new cinnamon clove mint charcoal-based organic tooth-paste and was told she shops at Afford-i-Mart. I'm deeply hurt and betrayed by the fact that CEO Jack Ripuoff has employed people who don't believe in the mission of healthy lifestyles enough to actually shop in the store that pays them! I hope @Jack Ripuoff will be more careful about who his stores hire in the future!

I click post. Within ten minutes, I've received fifty likes and ten, then fifteen, then twenty-five shares. Go, team!

I don't stop there. I tweet. I TikTok, I Insta, and even shoot a quick YouTube video.

"Healthy Mart is a huge chain with lots of devoted and loyal followers who shop there because we believe in the store's mission. Why shouldn't their employees be expected to do the same?

* * *

Maybe I overreacted, leaving my basket there in the aisle. A week has gone by and now I really need to top off my groceries. I was pleased to receive a Tweet reply from Jack Ripuoff, that was cool.

"I will look into this, thank you!" he posted.

Look into this. That could mean anything.

I contemplate going to their competitor, but I would have to drive an hour and that's a lot of work. So, I head back to Healthy Mart.

With my little basket almost filled, the only thing I need is aloe juice. I can't find it anywhere. Looking around to ask for directions, it seems there are fewer people on the floor than usual. It's not lunchtime. I wonder where everyone is.

"Excuse me?" I say approaching the Customer Service desk.

"Yes?" A woman whose tag identifies her as Rachel, replies.

"It seems to me there aren't as many associates on the floor today. Is something wrong?"

She looks uncomfortable suddenly. I hope I wasn't prying.

She leans over the counter and tells me, in a confidential tone, "We got a memo from corporate, had to institute a new policy that staff spends a certain amount of their check shopping here. To prove they align with the company mission. People who couldn't either quit or got fired."

She looks around as if she's just divulged a big secret.

"Well, that's good, right? I mean shouldn't employees prove they align with the values of the store?"

"You don't understand. Working here in and of itself proves this. They don't pay enough for the entry-level staff to afford to shop here. Heck, I've had to take a third job to be able to afford to follow this new initiative. Apparently, some crazy shopper complained all over the internet because she found out an employee didn't shop here. Now I'm stuck doing my job and the job of everyone who quit or got fired and on top of that, I'm losing most of my income to buy the groceries here. So much for sustainability."

# HELP WANTED

Wanted, a bright and innovative new talent to contribute to the IT operations of a burgeoning new corporation. FU Inc. is fast becoming one of the most competitive names in transportation. As we continue to grow, we're excited to bring new talent on board.

Who knows, maybe that's you!

If you're the perfect fit for our current vacancy, you have a bachelor's degree in Computer Science/Information Technology or related field with five years of experience in this field. Our ideal client also has experience in management and accounting. Ability to bake a souffle with a perfect fluffy texture is also preferred.

Our ideal candidate will also have a CDL Bus Driver's license and has experience as a licensed HAM Radio operator. Proficiency in ice skating and face painting are also encouraged.

In addition, we are keeping an eye out for a candidate knowledgeable in 1980s Broadway musicals. Take note, you may be asked to sing any number of selections from Andrew Lloyd Weber's greatest hits before our panel of highly discerning managers to be considered for this position.

**Your job duties will include but are not limited to:**

· Review diagnostics and assess the functionality and efficiency of systems.

· Implement security measures.

· Monitor security certificates and company compliance with requirements.

· Painting, decorating and fumigating offices as needed.

· Offer technical support to company staff and troubleshoot computer problems.

· Cleaning manager restrooms as requested.

· Maintain and supervise bus fleet including taking responsibility for ordering parts and repairing vehicles, as necessary.

We are offering a generous compensation package which includes $10.00/hourly salary with the potential for raise to $12.00/hour after 10 years of exceptional service. Paid Time Off is available through our crowdfunding app which you have access to after an initial 8-month probationary period.

# Killing Joe Bonvenuto

Today is Tuesday. It's time to kill Joe Bonvenuto. Again.

Just like Sunday, and Monday, and Wednesday. Jeremy kills him on Thursdays, Fridays, and Saturdays as well.

Not a day has gone by in the past two years that Jeremy has not, in some way shape, or form, killed Joe Bonvenuto. He's been kicked off of most blogging platforms, had a restraining order, and been issued fines.

"And the kicker is," Jeremy never misses the chance to tell people, "only one of us is an actual murderer."

Joe Bonvenuto is still alive. Jeremy's wife Alisha is not.

Jeremy sits at his laptop while his coffee sits in the microwave. Beep. Beep. Beep. It's ready. But not before his daily ritual.

He thinks of food and kitchens and posh country clubs like the one in Saratoga that he belongs to. Maybe today a line cook will slip a little rat poison into his Foie Gras. Yes. Yes, that's good.

He starts typing away. Once he gets going it doesn't take long. The means, the method, a quick spell check and submit.

He doesn't always even check the spelling.

With a click of the button, today's story of the killing of Joe Bonvenuto is published on about a dozen different online platforms.

Now it's coffee time.

* * *

"Don't you think you're keeping yourself stuck in the past by writing these violent stories every day?" the court-ordered therapist asks.

"What if I am? The past, the present, the future, they no longer exist. Everything I cared about is gone. What more do I have to do with my time but kill Joe Bonvenuto every day?"

"Wouldn't you rather at least try to move on? To be happy? Do meaningful things?"

Carla is dressed in a crisp new outfit. Jeremy notices that every week when he sees her, she always has a new outfit. She sits in her office with just the right amount of sunshine mixed with just the right amount of cheap art from Target. Wall stickers reminding him to Live, Laugh, Love, and one or two nick-knacks from a boutique. He thinks to himself that her choice in décor lets her pretend to be woke and support the fairly traded handicrafts by some group or another of exploited artisans in some country Jeremy's sure she's never visited.

His eyes wander to the clock. It's getting boring again. So, he decides to make this visit worth his time.

"Why, yes. Yes, Carla, I suppose you're right. Well, with all this time I spend writing about killing Joe Bonvenuto I could be out there bettering myself. I could take a class in bomb-making, for example, or chemistry. I could go out and try to meet people. Make new friends. Pay one of them to break his windpipe."

"Do I have to call in a pickup order?"

"Do you honestly think I'm going to do any of those things? If I was going to, I would have already. I've told you before, it suits me that he stays alive so I can haunt him with his possible deaths, every day."

"What if he's not even paying attention to you? Then it's all for nothing."

"For a psychologist, you've got no grasp on human motivation." He tells her. "He doesn't need another yacht. Or House. Or boat. Or business. Or suit. Or sportscar. He collects these toys to try to give his life some meaning. Why?"

She pauses and taps her pen on her notepad. Jeremy thinks she's waiting for him to answer.

"Because he's afraid of dying. It's the one thing he can't buy his way out of."

"So?"

"So? He dedicates his life to forgetting his mortality. And I'm dedicating the rest of my life to reminding him of it. Every day. You know what I did those two months they put me in jail for stalking him?"

"Same thing you do every day. Wrote stories about his death."

"I did, but then they took away my writing supplies and threw me in solitary. Which was even better. The guards who stood outside my cell heard a marathon. All-day, all night, with an hour or so here and there break when I fell asleep, they got the full narration of all the ways Joe Bonvenuto could die."

"What purpose did that serve?"

"Do you have kids?"

"Excuse me? That's not your business."

"True enough," Jeremy concedes. "But you know kids. You know little kids. If you ask them if Santa is real, they'll tell you he is. They'll tell you all the details about his reindeer and his workshop and his favorite cookies. Why?"

"Because they believe in him."

"Because they've heard the stories," he corrects her. "They've heard the stories over and over and over again. That's what makes it real. Those guards may never meet Bonvenuto. They've got it drilled in their heads. They heard his name thousands of times and if you hospitalize me or lock me up or stick me in the DMV for hours waiting to renew my license, no matter where I am I will circulate the stories of the one thing this man can't conquer."

"Do you think that's fair?"

"Why do the poor always have to play fair? Not people like Bonvenuto? Fuck your fair. He set the rules of this game when he got away with murder."

Jeremy recalls the hearing. All the OSHA citations. All the previous complaints. All the current and former employees who came forward, reluctantly, nonetheless. To say the same thing. Bonvenuto was responsible. Bonvenuto was negligent. Bonvenuto killed Alisha. But that wasn't what the judge said.

"Not guilty."

Even though Jeremy had produced emails. Alisha complaining not once, not twice, but five times, about the equipment not being safe. About the machine malfunctioning. All in the weeks leading up to her murder.

*And they tell me it was an accident.*

Carla's voice brings him back. She's on again about what is and isn't right. What is and isn't justice. What is and isn't fair.

They go back and forth like this for a while until relief comes over her face because once again our session is over. He wonders as he leaves her office if she realizes that she too has become a pawn in the game. If she knows that every week when she gives him a platform to kill Joe Bonvenuto again if she truly understands just how she is keeping the story going?

# CURSED

I roll the heavy window closed so the sound of my neighbor declaring war on the overnight trees in his yard won't interfere with the next call to come in. They've been relentless today.

"Thank you for calling Psychic Hotline, this is Giselda speaking. What would you like insight on today?"

"Hello, Giselda, my name is Tonya. I have to know if my luck is going to turn around soon. I haven't been able to find a job and I'm living in my car. I need to try to find something soon. Any luck for me? Lucky numbers maybe?"

My stomach sinks. I want to hang up on her. Or to tell her to get off the phone. To save her money for gas or food or a hotel room. But it's against company policy.

I would trade in fifty drunk people slurring in my ear about why he hasn't called back to not have someone living in their car ask me if their luck will change.

Luck has nothing to do with why Tonya has no home. I pull out cards one by one. Trying to come up with an eloquent yet accurate way to explain that she is wasting her money playing lottery as much as she's wasting it calling me.

Or looking for a job.

There is no "predatory capitalism" card. Well, not exactly.

"You will have other opportunities," I tell her the truth. What I don't tell her is that it will take three shit jobs to make enough to pay her half of the rent to split a one-bedroom apartment that isn't up to code.

"And I do see you finding a place within the month. It will be a start. Not ideal. But a start. Your money will come from three different sources."

"Lotto winnings one of them?"

"No, I would not count on that."

"Oh, ok. How about my modeling career?"

"Not in the near future. No. You'll need to piece it together with other options. Again, not ideal, but something."

"Well can't I just meet someone who has enough money to take care of me?"

"Theoretically yes, but this is not a good way to solve this problem."

She's mad now and yells at me for wasting her time. At least she hung up. At least she's saved whatever money is leftover and maybe will have some extra to eat. I know this isn't true. She'll call the next person on the line.

And another and another and another. Until one of the many psychics on the phone line tells her what she wants to hear. A few random numbers. Maybe once in a year, she'll win. Fifty dollars here. Maybe even a hundred there. Then she'll thank Psychic So-and-So who knew the magic winning numbers. Even though the person on the line likely had no idea what they were saying.

If they did, they wouldn't fill someone's head with the idea of lucky numbers. They wouldn't promise that the next guy she meets at a bar, a chance encounter, will be the one. That he has a name of (insert common man's name in her age group here) and that they will fall in love at first sight and move to the suburbs. They'll tell her that she's just about to land her dream job and that yes, her modeling career will take off. That within six months she'll be wealthy and have everything she wants.

That's what keeps them calling back and why I have so few repeat callers.

I can't fault the other psychics. For what we're paid, it's no wonder. The desperate prey on the even more desperate. A highly successful business model.

The phone rings again.

"Thank you for calling Psychic Hotline. This is Giselda speaking, what would you like insight on today?" It's been ten hours straight and I'm getting exhausted.

"Yes, I need you to tell me how to lift the curse that's been placed on me."

I roll my eyes.

There is no curse, but I humor the man and shuffle the cards. He's lost his job. Again. And it will be another year before he has solid work, through no fault of his own. Not for lack of trying.

"There's no curse on you. You've had a rough patch and the bad news is things will continue to be challenging. You'll have some work opportunities but not in line with your career path. Not until next March. But you're doing all you can do."

"Then why have I had all this bad luck?"

"You haven't had bad luck."

"What do you mean? I lost three jobs in a row. The company downsized, then another got bought out and the last one went out of business!"

Now he's getting mad.

"Why won't you tell me how to lift this curse?" He starts demanding, screaming into the phone. I've had enough.

"You want to know how to turn your bad luck around?" I ask, speaking his language.

"Yes, please!"

"First off, stop voting for people who sell out the working class. Second, go to the library and get yourself a copy of Howard Zinn's *A People's History of the United States.* Don't invest in corporations that exploit their workers and your next boss will be less likely to exploit you. When you find a politician, who is willing to stand up to Wall Street, instead of calling them a "commie," try supporting their campaign instead."

Silence. I continue.

"You're not cursed. The run of bad luck is all a natural consequence of living in an out-of-control capitalist system. We can drown in it, or we can fight back. Stop blaming supernatural forces for not having a reasonable standard of living while you throw all your power and autonomy away to the one percent who continue to rob you b-"

Dial tone.

# LEARNING DIVISION

1991

I don't like to leave the class, but I really have to pee, and I couldn't wait for lunchtime. Miss G. let me go to the bathroom. But one toilet is full of toilet paper. The other has a sign, 'out of order,' and someone is in the third stall.

I go to the principal's office.

"Hi, sweetie, what's up?" Mrs. W., the Principal's helper greets me. I tell her about the bathroom situation. "Why don't you go downstairs to the staff room and tell them I said you can use that bathroom, ok?"

I don't like to go in there. It smells like coffee and cigarettes. But I really have to pee. I nod my head and go downstairs.

"Mrs. W. said I could use the bathroom, because the girls' room stalls are full and out of order," I tell Mrs. R. who opens the door to the staff room for me. She points to the bathroom, and I hurry in.

It's boring in there, with nothing to read on the stalls while I take care of business so instead, all I have to do is listen to the teachers on break. Mrs. R. is talking to Mr. C.

That's when I hear it. Something awful has happened.

"They announced it this morning, on the radio, you knew it was just a matter of time." Mr. C. says.

My stomach feels sick now, but I can't go anymore. I flush and wash up. There's no mirror so I smoosh my eyes with my hands to make sure no tears are coming out.

My heart races as I walk back to class. Surely Miss G. didn't hear the news. She would have told us. Or we would be going home.

Mom and Dad always talk about the day Kennedy was killed. They announced it on the loudspeaker at V.I., where they went to school. Everyone got sent home early. Every old person knows where they were when Kennedy was killed and when they get together, they talk about it and compare notes.

This is just as bad. Maybe worse. I head toward the principal's office again. Maybe I should tell them so they can announce it on the loudspeaker like the pledge and then send everybody home. But I panic even more. My hands sweat. I don't want to tell the principal.

I head back to Miss G.'s class. I'll wait 'til break and then pull her aside and tell her so that she can tell everyone else.

I still can't believe it as I take my seat.

"Twelve, divided by six is…" I can't pay attention.

We've gone to war.

That's what Mr. C. said.

Ridiculous! We can't go to war. We already did that. And we won. Both my grandfathers were there. They both survived, but a lot of other people died, so that's how everyone decided not to do that again and they made something called the UN, which is what you put in front of words to undo something.

The UN undoes war.

That's what we pay them taxes for, dad says. And Uncle Joe says he's tired of paying taxes for socialism and then they argue, and I join in, on Dad's side and Grammy threatens to call the cops.

You can't undo the UN because it includes people from the whole world.

And even with the UN, we had another war, Vietnam. It's in all the movies. And when old people talk about Kennedy dying, they also talk about Vietnam.

But they all agree Vietnam was a mistake and it was only rich people sending poor people to fight and so everybody protested and burned flags and eventually the war ended.

So now the UN should really have gotten the message because they know what happens when you go to war by mistake.

"Brian!" Miss G. yells at one of my classmates, I startle to attention and look toward the board, trying not to look at Brian who just got yelled at again. My eyes sting again, Miss G. keeps yelling at Brian, "if you don't pay attention, you're going to make mistakes and you'll have to repeat this!"

Exactly! I want to yell. We can't be repeating it. We already made that mistake about war and we're good now.

My hands get even more sweaty, and I wonder how late in the war we are. If the airplanes will drop bombs right now, while Miss G. talks about division. A bomb may hit before I get a chance to tell her.

"Declared war with the Middle East. This Morning." Mr. C. had said.

I know east. That's across the river. Our friend Jeff moved to Troy and when we went to visit, I asked Mom where we were going and she said about twenty minutes east, to Troy. Troy looked nice. With old buildings and a park. There's also East

Greenbush and Rensselaer. I don't know which one is in the middle.

It occurs to me then that I don't know who to look out for. If we're at war with the Rensselaer or East Greenbush or Troy, we all pretty much look and talk the same. Or close enough. People on that side of the river could basically be people from Albany. You can't tell.

But then I remember gym class, how we wear tunics to show who is on what team for dodgeball. So, they'll probably pick a tunic and that's how we'll know who to fight with or hide from.

"And that is how you divide." Miss G. puts down her chalk and wipes the dust from her hands in a "that's that," motion.

"Now, are there any questions?"

I have a lot of questions. Why did we declare war on Troy? Are tanks going to roll down the streets? Is there still a draft?

My dad never finished college. He got drafted. But then his vision was bad, so they didn't let him fight anyway but he never went back to school. My vision starts to go bad. I can't see the board. Maybe I won't have to get drafted. But it's not the same. It's just tears. I smoosh my eyes shut and pretend like I have an itch.

Miss G. announces break time. We'll wash our hands and then have a snack. We're allowed out of our seats to get in line, but I don't get in line. I walk up to her; afraid she may yell at me for not being in line. But it doesn't matter because I have to tell her.

"Miss G.?"

She turns toward me and scowls but doesn't yell. "Yes?"

"I have something to tell you."

We aren't sent home early.

"There won't be any fighting here. Only in the Middle East."

Turns out it's not the other side of the river. It's the other side of the ocean. So, it's pretty far away. Our troops will go there to drop bombs and fight in the streets.

"Won't their troops come here to drop bombs?" I ask.

"No, it doesn't work that way."

"Don't they have airplanes?"

"Yes, they do."

"Then what stops them from bringing their bombs here too?"

"They can't do that."

I don't understand. It doesn't seem fair to fly somewhere else and drop bombs but not allow other people to bomb you back. It's like on the playground when some of the kids throw stones but if you throw stones back you get in trouble. If anyone is going to throw stones or drop bombs, then everyone should be allowed to. Or else no one should do it.

Which is what I thought the UN decided. But not anymore.

The UN gave permission. So, it must be like when you're not really supposed to do something but then Mom gets tired of hearing you beg so she lets you. The UN must have gotten tired of hearing President Bush beg to go to war, so they aren't stopping him. So much for the UN.

"But why are they doing this?"

No one explains a reason. They tell us it will likely be a small war. A short war. Nothing like WWII or Vietnam. There are new technologies. They will only hit their exact targets. No one else will get hurt.

I don't believe it.

I don't know why the same people who agreed Vietnam was a mistake think this war is ok. Why would anyone think it's ok? Didn't they watch MASH?

For our assignment, we are each given a pen pal in the army and we're going to write letters to cheer them up and thank them.

I don't know what we are thanking them for.

I stare at my paper, imagining a school in the Middle East. Wondering if the buildings look like the buildings in our east, Troy, East Greenbush, and Rensselaer. I don't have anything to say, so I ask questions.

"Why are you there? Did you have to kill anyone? How did you know you killed the right person? Why is there a war? Do you even like President Bush?"

Then I get ideas. I tell my pen pal how I don't like President Bush and how my uncle does. How when we all get together for dinner, my dad and me get into fights with my uncle, who is a republican, and we yell and curse, and then Grammy threatens to call the police. I tell him how Bush is greedy, like Reagan and all the corporations. I tell him I hope he doesn't get shot and that it really would be better if he didn't bomb anyone.

People put yellow ribbons out for the troops as a sign of good luck, like a rabbit's foot. Suddenly, everyone is wearing American Flags. Miss G. scolds Tom for wearing an American Flag on his shorts because it's against the law.

I don't know why it is legal to bomb people but not legal to wear a flag on your clothes.

People also talk about Saddam. Now, even if you didn't like President Bush before, you're supposed to pretend to like him, or else you're not patriotic. It's ok to joke about bombing Saddam because Saddam's people don't like him.

But I don't like President Bush, and if I joke about bombing President Bush, I get in trouble.

Bette Midler sings a song on the radio about how God is watching us, from a distance.

Maybe He has to keep a distance, so he doesn't get bombed by accident.

# LONG DIVISION

## 2001

Class ended early. Social Psychology. Professor walked in, not realizing the severity of what had just happened. She made a joke. Then the head of the Psych department knocked on the door and said all classes were dismissed. There would be a debriefing in the Auditorium for anyone who wanted to attend.

It's eerily silent as I walk through the dorm. The doors that are open reveal TVs all repeating the same news.

One plane. Then another.

People gather around and cry and stare at the screen. Class didn't end early when we started bombing the Middle East, but someone finally attacked us back.

It's the anniversary of the day we killed Allende, but we won't call it that. From now on, we'll just call it 9/11 and it will be all about us.

"Here comes the war. Here come the yellow ribbons. Here come the crackdowns." I tell my roommate.

I've seen this movie before.

\* \* \*

2007

It's freezing when I board the bus. I soon regret wearing layers. As we leave the Capitol Region and get closer to DC the sun comes out in full force. It's late January, but that means it's in the mid-50s in D.C. I didn't know this. I've never been here before. Most of the people on the bus are older.

They were sent home when JFK was shot. They were drafted or burned flags and protested Vietnam. Where were they when we declared war in 91? Some of them protested, no doubt. But how many put yellow ribbons on their trees?

Quakers, Mothers, Friends, and Neighbors for Peace. Veterans Against War, they have different buttons and stickers. Some brought signs. I didn't think a sign would fit on the bus.

At the bus station, I try to pay attention to where we're dropped off. We chartered a bus together, but I'm not with any group. And we aren't the only bus. Hundreds of people are filling the streets. We walk toward the Capitol. Homeless people are face down on the ground. I don't have anything to give.

I've been to protests before. Nothing like this. There are thousands of people here. I don't have a cell phone. I don't have a camera. Others are filming. Some people hand out signs. I take one that is offered. A "W" with a circle and line through it on one side. End This War on the other side.

There are speakers and musicians but I'm too far away to hear them. I walk with the marchers. A line of people dressed in black with bandanas over their faces come through. Some have Guy Fawkes masks on. They drum and dance and perform street theater. I learn later they are called Antifa.

We march and chant and I know it will have little impact. The war will continue. The government has gotten better at ignoring people. No one wants to up the ante.

The next day I see news coverage online. Of all the people from every state who gathered peacefully, of all the speakers, for all the importance of the message: End this war, there is one repeated headline.

*Protesters descend on Capitol, leave trash behind.*

# Poorest House in a Rich Neighborhood

*Can be read as a poem aloud in your own voice or sung in your mind to the tune of the average Blink-182 song.

It's the poorest house in a rich neighborhood
    He wants to make it his own
    Because it feels so good

To finally know every privilege, he never earned
    And a few years of work
    Have improved his net worth

All the battles his granddad and father fought for
    Him to carry his wife
    Across the doorway

Of the poorest house
    In the rich neighborhood.

And it didn't quite cost a half a million dollars
    So, he'll put in an indoor pool, in-law house, and a sauna
    Build a three-season room

With someone else's labor
Then maybe he'll find it worthwhile to stay there

He says he came from humble beginnings
    But he's spent his life so busy winning
    Never stopped to wonder why the tenants paying
    For his lifestyle could never live
    In even the poorest house
    In a rich neighborhood
    Like his.

Well, that's the problem with a capitalist
    Born under the sign of Sagittarius
    He pretends to be one of the Proletariat
    But he sold his tenants out to a plutocrat
    And he's got class traitors tricks to pull out of his hat
    To keep him in the poorest house
    In a rich neighborhood.

No, he won't get invited to the finest boat parties
    But he tries to tell himself he's just getting started
    He tells them give it time, he's got upward mobility
    But he can't see
    He's thrown his life into trying to be
    One of the wealthy elites
    When he could have just been
    A decent person of means
    Helping to raise the floor under his feet
    In solidarity

With other working people

But it's too late now
 He's pledged allegiance to the house
 That costs the least in the town
 That costs the most

The poorest house
 In the rich neighborhood.

# SETTLED

She resets the needle again. The grandkids would tease her if they were here. But she can't help it. She likes the sound of the scratch before the melody starts. Before George Jones announces the news about a man professing love until death.

She sips her tea. It's getting cold. Maybe she'll wear down the record before she finishes her cup. Oh well.

Settling back into her worn recliner, she hears the trucks pulling through. The last of her neighbors packing. Moving.

"Where you moving to?" Ginny had asked her yesterday evening.

"Not moving." She had simply said in reply.

"Did Bonvenuto make a deal? To let you stay here? That's great if he did!"

"No. Heartless sonofabitch making no deals."

"What are you going to do?" Ginny had asked.

"I'll sit on my ass, drink tea. And listen to records."

*And here I am.*

She remembers how Ginny had looked at her then, like the way you look at someone who has lost their marbles, but you don't want to let on that you know. Like she was handling the older woman. But I got my marbles, she thinks. For now.

"What are they going to do? Kill me?" she had laughed to her daughter, on the line from Seattle. She sounded worried.

*Probably thinks I have Old Timers.*

"Mom, you have to start looking for a place!"

She remembers how in a panic; she had begun yelling. Got mouthy. That's ok.

George Jones's voice fills the room, reminding her that now, he's over her for good. The chorus begins again.

*Put a wreath around my door, Georgie, I'm done,* she thinks to herself.

She sips her peppermint tea, and it gives her heartburn. She throws it across the room. The cup smashes, peppermint scent fills the room. And George keeps singing.

She laughs.

Because no one can tell her not to.

Because what's a fucking teacup when you've nothing more to lose?

*It just missed your picture, too Hank.* She thinks, looking at the photo from when he was in the service.

She keeps his pictures up, just like he always liked them. Didn't pack a thing. Nothing of ours going into a box, she says out loud, with only the record to respond.

She looks at the photo on the end table, the one she keeps close by. Their wedding day. Who'd have thought, way back then? She wonders. Over forty years ago now. When this would just be a pit stop on the way to the next big thing.

When this trailer was the best they could do. And it wasn't bad. Newer model back then. When there was still time to think things would eventually get better.

She stares fondly at the photo and can see the pride in his face. How he grinned ear to ear like he'd won the lottery.

If only.

And she couldn't fit my arm into the dress she wore. Hard to believe the woman with that face was her, she thinks.

She reaches for the record player and resets the needle. Her arm bumps the photo as she does. She resets it perfectly.

Perfect. As it had been.

Before the plant shut down. Before his accident at the next job. Before the kids. Before the recession, inflation, stagflation, damnation.

*And suddenly you were gone.*

The kids, grown.

And nothing left but the home they never got to launch from.

It served them well, she supposes. She eyes the yellowed wallpaper. Always hated the stuff. The curtains, popular probably thirty years ago. The floors, permanently stained in ways that defy any amount of bleach and elbow grease.

Like a captain resigned to sink with the ship, she smiles and admires the mementos that, like her, will have no other home.

The trophies from bowling league. The kids' school and prom and then wedding photos. The newspaper clipping from that time her husband helped save a kid who nearly drowned over at Saratoga Lake.

She thinks of how he always hated that she had had it framed.

She needs reminders of integrity. That good people existed. Once.

George Jones reminds her that it won't be long until they carry him away.

Again.

*They can carry me away. If that's what they want to do.*

The song finishes again. She reaches to reset the needle. A sharp rap on the door startles her. She drops the needle and knocks over their wedding photo.

*He said I'll ....*

*He said I'll ...*

*He said I'll ...*

She sets the needle and George completes his verse.

"Who is it?" She calls. Knowing damn well who it is.

"Saratoga County Sheriff. Looking for Ms. Josephine Turley."

"Mrs."

"Sorry, Mrs. Turley, is that you?"

The voice calls from the other side of the door. Competing with my record.

"Mrs. Turley, please open the door."

"Go fuck yourself, Sheriff," she replies, crossing her fingers over her belly, sitting back in her chair.

"Mrs. Turley, I'm here to serve you with an eviction."

"Well then do it. Then go fuck yourself."

George's voice carries through the trailer. As he sings the title line of the song, He Stopped Loving Her Today, the floor vibrates from the sound.

Just as well. She didn't want to listen to him hounding her anyway.

"Mrs. Turley, open the door."

"Or else what?"

Bored already with him, she opens her library book. It's a good one. About a man who travels back in time to prevent the Kennedy assassination. Clever. She wishes she could go back in time. She imagines going back to the early eighties and giving Roger Ailes a papercut.

"Mrs. Turley, we need you to open the door!"

"And I need some chocolate and a good hot orgasm. Take a number!"

"Mrs. Turley, please!"

She tries to ignore the voice, opting instead to hear George say, once again, that they've put a wreath on his door.

"What do you want?" She finally responds to the incessant banging.

"We're here to evict you!"

"Well. it's not going to work from the other side of the door, now is it precious? You weren't top of your class, were you?"

She turns the pages, idly. No longer focusing on the book. Or on the record. He's ruined her afternoon.

"Mrs. Turley, you no longer have authorization to be here."

"Well, you never did, so now we're a team."

"Mrs. Turley, if you don't open this door by the count of three, I'm going to force entry and remove you from the premises."

"Whatever blows up your tights, darling."

He counts down as she rolls her eyes and chuckles. Then the banging begins again. It doesn't take much effort to break the door down.

"Mrs. Turley, we will remove you from the premises by force if you don't go voluntarily."

She looks briefly in the direction of the door. The loudmouth Sheriff is joined by a few other cops, standing farther back on the front deck.

"I'm not leaving. This was not my choice. I'm going nowhere."

He tries to stare her down.

She smiles and resets the record.

*He said–*

"Mrs. Turley, don't make this harder than it has to be."

"I'm not doing anything. That's the point, son."

He turns toward his backup and then looks back at her.

"We're very busy today."

"No kidding. You have a lot of people to throw out on the street, do you?"

"Mrs. Turley…"

"What part of my statement was inaccurate?"

"Mrs. Turley where are your bags? Pack your bags. It's time to go. You had a warning."

"I'm not leaving. That's my warning to you."

"Is that a threat?"

"Oh yes son, be afraid of me." She cackles and judging by the look on his reddening face, can tell it's getting under his skin.

He motions to his crew, and they surround her. Another warning. Then another. Then another. They grab her arms.

"I'm not leaving!" She screams.

They pull her to her feet. She drops her weight to the floor. They start to drag her. She holds on to whatever she can reach. First the table. The record begins to skip again as, in the scuffle, she pulls the table a few feet.

*He stopped–*

*He stopped–*
*He stopped–*

Her wedding photo crashes to the ground, glass shattering in all directions.

A cop curses.

They try to heave her forward again. She grabs the bottom of the couch. She doesn't recall much of the next part of the scuffle.

She knows that when her daughter, her former neighbors, her friends, read about it in the paper, they'll be shocked. She was shocked too, didn't plan on biting one of them in the shins until the opportunity presented itself. Like a dog. It felt good, she thinks. She bit him hard.

She grabs for his gun, the last thing she hears is George crooning that he's over her for good this time.

\* \* \*

The record, still a vinyl parrot, echoes again and again, he's over her for good.

"Damn, will you shut that thing off while I call for an ambulance?" Sheriff Wilbur barks at Officer Timmons.

"Whatever you say, boss." He looks confused. Like he's never seen one of these before. Eventually, he figures it out.

"Yeah, It's Sheriff Wilbur. We're here serving evictions and there was an incident. Going to need an ambulance. It doesn't look good. Better send the coroner. Yep. Yep, it was a suicide. Older woman. Must have been mentally ill."

# The Secret of Your Success

## Jayden

I stole Grandma's credit card to hire the Lyft driver. Grandma can afford the fare and a big tip. Fifty percent. He pulls up to the sign for the Saratoga Country Club and Golf Course. I thank my driver, Jason, for the ride as I close the car door.

"Have a good day at work!"

I smile and nod. I've got a job to do here today, so technically I wasn't lying about that part. I sweep the little specs of light dog hair off my pants.

"Buddy's a Golden Retriever," Jason told me when I got into the car.

No, I'm not allergic. Yes, I have a dog too. No, he's a pit mix. We made the normal small talk.

If I'm going to pretend to be here for work, I can't go in wearing little pieces of Buddy on my black pants, though. The same pants I wore to Mom's funeral last week. The thought flies into my mind and I push it down, so it can't sink in. As long as I don't think about it for too long, it won't be real. Mom will still be at rehab. Which is where she was.

"Getting better every day, babe!"

The last time I spoke to her on the phone.

Getting better. Taking a break from all the stress. That's what her counselor told Grandma and Danny and me. "We can start allowing family phone calls, but it's important to not bring up anything stressful right now."

The sun is already high in the sky. I feel my body getting sweaty under my only nice dress shirt. I hope I don't end up with nasty pit stains, but the long road to the country club is out in the full sun, no shade, no way to cool off.

My feet kick up dust as I walk the path toward the enormous building where the event is taking place. I found out about it online. Just like how I find out about everything else. What else do I have to do?

"We're all going to be home soon," Mom said on that last phone call.

Did I tell her I love her? Or did I just say "uh-huh" and then hand the phone to Grandma? I didn't pay attention enough to remember. If I had known it would be the last phone call, I would have paid more attention. I would have talked to her longer. I would have hung up on Mom before letting Grandma talk to her.

But I didn't know.

Because Mom was getting better.

Is getting better, I correct myself. Because she's still alive. She's still in rehab. She's coming home soon.

I recite the script in my head, knowing none of it is true. If it was true, I wouldn't be here. Watching as the country club looms larger, distorted by mirage lines in the sun.

I feel the stabbing in my heart again. Lump in my throat. Tears in my eyes. No crying at work, I remind myself. I'm here to do my job.

I switch to the other script. The one I practiced just for today.

\* \* \*

## Joe Bonvenuto

The limo pulls up and I tell my assistant to tip the driver, but only five percent. Don't want him getting too full of himself. Marcy, my assistant, and Dora, my wife, and I step out of the Limo. I stretch my legs and take off the ridiculous mask so I can take in some nice, clean, golf course air.

Bobby Walton meets us at the door.

"Joe! Great to see you again! Congratulations on your award."

"Thanks, Bobby."

We shake hands and shoot the shit. Dora and Marcy catch up with me. I can tell by the pout on Dora's face she's not happy, but it's been a few months since she brought up that crap about the affair with Marcy. I assume she's over it. Mostly. Still, it isn't lost on me that she purposely stands as close to me as she can, pushing Marcy off to the side in her subtle way.

So, this is how today's going to be.

We've had a talk about this already. About today being a photo op.

*Don't embarrass me, Dora.* I made it clear before we left the house. As soon as Bobby walks us through the restaurant and out to the back patio, she forgets all about her little jealousy and heads right for the open bar.

Out in the back, the garden and patio are decorated with the colors and logo for the Center for the Prevention of Child Trafficking. Yellow and navy blue. Not my favorite color combo, but all things considered, they've done a decent job.

I've been to a million of these over the years and after a while, it starts to become like being invited to weddings. The first few are exciting, but after a dozen or so it just becomes a nuisance. Bad music, mediocre trendy food, and a reason to have to throw away perfectly good money on a new suit I'll only wear once. Truth be told, I'd rather be out golfing or fishing on the lake. But being the recipient of the inaugural award from the Center for the Prevention of Child whatever they're calling it, it wouldn't look good if I don't show up.

Might as well come have a few drinks, some slightly bleeding steak, and smile for the cameras. Get my award, which will probably get stashed in a box somewhere or maybe at one of the boat storage units- customers love shit like that- and make it worth all the money I shelled out fundraising for them last year.

Bobby offers me a drink.

I guess they didn't spare any expenses, I think, facetiously as I have another sip of cognac.

One of the girls walks by, looks like she just ran a marathon. I swear, they must be hiring anyone off the streets these days.

"You there, young lady," I snap my fingers to get her attention.

She looks at me, surprised at first. Like she forgot what her job is. Then, something else passes over her face. Can't put my finger on it, but it's already gone. She blinks twice and then says, "uh, yeah?"

Who talks to a guest like that? I'm going to talk to Scottie, the manager, and recommend more training on customer service.

"The appropriate response," I reply, "would be 'yes,' or even 'yes, Sir.' Now you try it."

"Yes, Sir?" she parrots back, but she says it with a look on her face like she's smelling shit.

"You need to work on that. In the meantime, get us each a Mint Julep."

He turns to his friend and continues, "Just like old times, right Bobby?"

Bobby smiles and nods as he downs the last of his cognac.

"Right away," she says, and hurries off in the opposite direction from the bar.

"What was that all about?" Bobby asks.

"You just can't find good help these days. These kids are all so entitled. I'm going to talk to Scottie about it."

"All the business you give this place, you definitely should. Have that girl fired if she isn't back with our drinks in five minutes, too!"

We talk and stroll outdoors- it's a perfect day- and peruse the hors d'oeuvres.

"Joe! It's great to see you!" Shelley from the Saratoga Digest comes in for a hug, as usual. She smells like old lady perfume, aging herself at least thirty years, also as usual.

"Great to see you too, Shelley."

As we pick from among the salmon and cream cheese puff and charcuterie spread, she's the first to bring up the inevitable.

"Not to bring up gloomy topics, Joe but you literally dodged a bullet! How are you feeling?"

She mentions this as if somehow I've forgotten.

"Well, I've had to increase the security around our home. And the lake house and summer home in Florida for good measure. Aside from that, I'm fine. Probably hurt my wallet more than it hurt me!"

She and Bobby chuckle.

"I'm glad they got that loon. What an awful thing! Have you had any more trouble from the white trash in that park?"

"No, no trouble at all. In a few months, they won't be my problem anymore."

"Ah, and then you'll be hearing the sound of bulldozers?" Bobby pipes in.

"And cash registers." I raise my glass and wink. The three of us toast as we balance our little snack plates. Shelley drops a stuffed shrimp on the lawn. We laugh as she uses the back of her shoe to shove it under the table, so it won't be in the way.

"I want to catch up with you for an interview before the event's over, Joe," she says, then runs her finger down my tie, gives me a wink, and heads off to mingle with the other guests.

As the place fills up, I'm bombarded. Knew this would happen. Everyone asking the same questions and the same bad puns about dodging bullets. They say there's no such thing as bad publicity, but I can do without constant reminders of that afternoon.

And where the hell is that girl with my drink?

\* \* \*

## Jayden

I knew him as soon as I saw him. He's even uglier in person. Sure, I'll get you a Mint Julep. Shove it up your ass. But of course, I didn't say that. I just kept to the background, blended in the best I could with the other staff. Took a few old ladies' coats to the coatroom, helped a few people find the restroom. Refilled some waters and waited.

Even pretending to work here is hard work. My feet are killing me, and I can't sit down because no one who works here is sitting down, so I would definitely draw attention to myself if I did that, even for a minute. But as the crowd picks up all the chaos and running here and there makes the time fly.

And then the ceremonies begin.

I try to listen to the boring speeches droning on and on, while also dodging the demands made by balding men who try to flirt with me and women wearing so much makeup, it looks like they took lessons from an undertaker.

Undertaker.

I try not to hear our last conversation, or what Grandma said when she got the phone.

"You got another letter from that Bonvenuto guy.... Well, what are you going to do about it? Your whole family is about to be homeless, and you're off in some rehab only thinking about yourself!"

I shake the scene away.

The woman in the casket didn't look like Mom at all. More proof she's not really dead. Still at rehab. Getting better.

I hover close to the stage. Refilling water. Taking orders, I have no intention of fulfilling. Keeping an ear out.

Some senator rambles about how important the Center for the Prevention of Child Trafficking was in helping his campaign to look for some missing girl about thirty years ago. He says they never found her, so more likely it helped his campaign to get re-elected.

Applause from the audience followed by some guy in a ridiculous top hat who says he's on the board at NYRA. Looking around, I'm sure half these people are. They laugh at his attempts at jokes, clap when expected to. All following the same script. Of course.

One by one, people I've never heard of take the stage and speak about what a hero Bonvenuto is. An asset to the community. A successful businessman. A philanthropist. A local treasure. The worst is when they keep talking about the "secret to his success." Makes me want to vomit. I wonder when they're going to just cut to the chase and lick his asshole. It would save a lot of time and then we could all just have dessert.

Finally, a guy who introduces himself as the president of the Center for Prevention of Child Trafficking takes the stage. I recognize his name from the website. One of the many websites I scoured on sleepless nights since Mom has been dea-

In rehab, getting better.

The site where she saw the announcement for this event and this bullshit award.

I quietly put the jug of water I've been carrying on a table, sliding it over and knocking a plate of something that looks like a yeast infection on little crackers off to the side. Some of the yeast infection crackers fall to the ground. No one notices. They're watching the stage.

I scale the steps and walk onto the stage. It's warm out, but I feel like the sun just got hotter. I feel myself sweating profusely now. Heart pounding. The director doesn't see me at first. Then he does. He looks confused, then alarmed.

I take advantage of his shocked reaction and pull the mic from his hand before he can figure out what to do with me.

I don't have long, after what happened at the Starbucks, there's security everywhere. I face the audience.

"You're here because you care about children," I begin, "My name is Jayden and I'm fourteen years old. My family lives… lived in a trailer in a park that he's destroying!" I point to Bonvenuto, in the front row, like a witness in a courtroom calling out a guilty defendant.

Yes, Your Honor, he's the one who did it…

The whispers in the crowd die down. They're watching. Uncomfortable, angry, shocked, but they're watching. I don't have much time. The news is here. Channels 10 and 13. I see cell phones go up, people in the back and sides of the courtyard taking video. Mostly other employees.

"You're not a hero! You don't care about children! You're about to make children homeless! Me, my brother Danny, he's only nine, our neighbor Grafton, he's eight. You don't care about kids! You just want to dress up and get your picture taken and pretend you're something when you ain't shit!"

There's a rustling in the crowd. Security is making their way from all directions.

"You're sixty-six years old! You've already sold a business and you have four other boat storage units, why do you need another? You've got a grandson in the Berkshires. How would you feel if your son's landlord threw them out of the house because he wanted the land for his business? You don't care about children!"

One of the security guards rushes the stage now and grabs for the mic. I lunge in the other direction and avoid his grasp, but I don't have long.

"You're all a bunch of phonies! Every one of you! Tell them the truth about your secret to success, Bonvenuto! You made your money by being a heartless dick!"

Someone does grab the mic from my hand then. I don't care. I've said what I needed to say. But I'm still not done. Another guard lifts me up and starts to carry me away. I keep screaming.

"You don't care about children, Bonvenuto! You're making us homeless! You're just a greedy scumbag! Go to Hell, all of you!"

Guards surround him and I hear some of the guests murmuring as I'm carried out of the pavilion. One of the guests, a man about Mom's age…

Because she's in rehab, getting better…

Points a finger at me and tells me I'm a disgrace. I cough hard and spit at his feet. Outside the gate, the guards throw me on the ground. Cops are waiting. I can't hear what they're saying.

My work is done.

Angela Kaufman is an astrologer, intuitive Tarot reader, writer, author and activist. Previous works of fiction include *Quiet Man* (2020) and *Golden Apple* (2021). She has also written several nonfiction books in the spirituality genre. Angela is a member of the IWW.

www.ingramcontent.com/pod-product-compliance
Lightning Source LLC
Chambersburg PA
CBHW020741130626
46554CB00006B/2088